OPERATOR 5:
LEGIONS OF THE DEATH MASTER

LEGIONS OF THE DEATH MASTER

By Curtis Steele

STEEGER BOOKS • 2020

CHAPTER 1
AMBASSADORS OF DOOM

WITHIN HEARING of the Capitol building, in Washington, D.C., the voice of a mob rose with an ominous roar.

Anger rang from the throats of the hundreds of men crowding around the open truck on which a wild-eyed man was shouting, gesturing, exhorting them with passionate fervor. They raised shaking fists and muttered surly agreement to the speaker's rousing plea. From the surrounding streets scores of other men came to strengthen the mounting emotional furor. Over the gathering dark cloud of malevolent faces the inciting voice shrilled again and again.

"We are Americans who go hungry, whose families starve, who beg for pennies to buy bread, while millions pour into the war-chests of the militarists! The last war is not yet paid for, and the bloody generals are emptying our Treasury to finance the next. There, in that building, lies the greatest store of gold in the world—gold to buy us the food we're starving for, gold denied us but stuffed into the pockets of the war-makers for their asking! Americans, we must stand together in the war against war!"

Again the wrathful voice of the mob roared. Again and again men harried to listen, drawn into the maelstrom of rising black fury. Within the shadow of the Capitol the voices beat like a surf—waves of wrath rolling in from the sea of public opinion.

"Fight the war against war!"

"Stand together for peace!"

"Gold for the hungry—no gold for guns!"

"Feed the starving—not the cannon!"

A young man strode quietly toward the edge of the growing crowd while the howl dinned in his ears. Clean-cut, sharp-eyed, alert, he paused to study those giving growling support to the

LEGIONS OF THE DEATH MASTER

Utter disaster descended upon the War Building at the stroke of twelve!

inflammatory speaker. His face was that of an American, while in the mob were scores of faces of foreign cast. His were finely turned; but among the hundreds were many that were evil and malevolent. He had a mind that functioned coolly, keenly; theirs were minds swayed by the florid eloquence of any speaker last to address them.

They were a mere mob. He was the ace undercover agent of the United States Government—Operator 5.

A dark light came into his eyes as he listened. He saw eyes reflecting threats, heard mouths muttering surly maledictions, sensed savage ruthlessness in the air. He looked upon men whom he knew to be without mercy, without scruples—men as merciless as barbarians in the jungle.

Killers—cheering the plea for peace at any price!

Operator 5—Jimmy Christopher to those who knew him—turned thoughtfully from the mob as an angry mutter swept through it again. The resentful outbreak was caused by the voice of a second speaker carrying through the night, conflicting with the snarling pronouncements of the wild-eyed man on the truck. Not a hundred yards away another crowd was gathered, listening to another plea. Toward the second Operator 5 moved quietly, disturbed by the tightening tension in the air.

The second group was smaller, quieter. Within it Jimmy Christopher noted serious-faced men listening with grave attention. Many of them were well-dressed men of business, or connected with federal works, who had paused on their way home from a long day's work, to give serious consideration to the speaker's message. There was no fanaticism in the voice of the alert-eyed man who was speaking to them so earnestly.

"We face a crisis and we must face facts! Let those who wish to remain blind turn from the idea that steel is the magic wand of peace. Let us realize that steel must be our strength!"

JIMMY CHRISTOPHER noted that the speaker's hands were gripped white on the staff of a scythe. Its long, curved, gleaming blade sparkled sharp in the street-lights. Toward the glinting point of steel the solemn eyes of the crowd turned.

"With steel we harvest the grain that makes our daily bread. In the fields scythes swing—blades of steel—working to feed us. In the mills, wheels of steel grind the grain into flour. On the steel rails of America steel cars speed to carry it into our homes. Our food comes of steel, our shelter comes of steel—our national safety comes of steel. With steel we must arm ourselves! With weapons of steel for defense we must save ourselves from the scorn of the world—save ourselves from being a weakling among strong nations!"

Now, to the surprise of Operator 5, an angry mutter swept through the crowd. Turning, he saw men shouldering toward the platform. They were not the quiet-mannered, serious-faced audience drawn by an intelligent consideration of the speaker's message. They were ugly, burly, sinister figures whose very presence brought a sense of danger. They had come, Jimmy Christopher realized, from the other crowd, and they brought again to his mind a sinister word—killers.

"It means war!" one of them snarled.

"Buying arms means war!"

"Cannon for legal murder!"

"Bayonets for butchering our families!"

"It's our money—we say no!"

His nerves tensing, Operator 5 realized that this was a manifestation of a strife that was sweeping across the nation. This conflict of voices and clashing of purposes symbolized a vital issue confronting the American people—a problem on which the very destiny of the nation rested, and at this very hour. At a thousand points in the Capital the minds of men were battling with the issue clashing at this spot tonight. In every home was reflected the bitter controversy dealing with weapons of war—a war hanging imminent tonight over the entire world.

The DEATH SCYTHE

Snarling voices rising out of the crowd spoke a threat of spreading national turmoil.

"The United States has got to lead the world and disarm!"

"Fatten the munitions makers while we starve?—No!"

"Steel for ploughshares—not swords!"

On the platform the speaker faced the heckling grimly, his hands curled around the staff of the scythe. He raised it high, and its long, curved blade glittered again in the lights of the street.

"Let us forge honor and peace out of steel!"

"Steel—means—death!"

The hoarse, shouted answer brought a hush over the crowd. On its outer edges men began to drift away warily. Operator 5 stood his ground, sensing rising danger. The cry was echoed gutturally in the crowd as more and more of the evil-faced men pushed toward the platform.

"Steel means death!"

"Get down!"

"You're through talking!"

"We'll show you what steel's for!"

"Steel means death!"

STARTLED, OPERATOR 5 glimpsed a glitter of steel—an ominous glint which did not come from the scythe in the grasp of the speaker. It reflected from a long-bladed knife in the big hand of one of the advancing, malevolent-eyed men. Another flash followed—the street-light striking a reflection from a drawn gun. Quickly, anxiously, Operator 5 began shouldering toward the platform. His voice rang clearly:

"Go to your homes! You're in danger! Withdraw before—"

A roar of wrath rose to drown out his words—a thunderstorm of voices which broke suddenly. Out of the tempest of snarling words, lightning flashed—the lightning of gun-fire. Flame spat, a bullet whined across the platform, glass crashed across the street. The report was a signal which transformed the crowd into a stampeding mob stirred into terror by the threatening snarls and thrusts of the evil-faced men.

Onto the small portable platform of the speaker these savage destroyers crowded. Again a revolver spat; in several upraised hands keen-bladed knives flashed. Out of the turmoil came a groan as a blade swept downward. Among the trampling feet sounded a cry of mortal agony as a well-dressed man fell with blood spurting across his face from a bullet-hole in his forehead. Shrilly, in the surrounding darkness, a police whistle blasted—and the storm of voices broke anew.

Operator 5 sprang close to the platform. His hand darted to a raised arm driving a knife. His fingers clamped tightly on hard muscles, twisted sharply.

7

A savage snarl tore from the thick lips of the man with the knife as Operator 5's quick strategy wrested it away. He side-stepped a powerful blow, drove out a straight-armed answer: knuckles which smacked between glaring eyes. He leaped again, snatched at a gun, swiftly, desperately, tore it loose and leaped back.

Now the corner was a turmoil of terror. Men were running every which way. On the far sidewalks women screamed as they saw fear-whitened faces streaked with blood. Again and again the police whistles shrilled, and toward the spot the Capital police came rushing.

Operator 5 saw the evil-faced men scattering, echoing warnings to each other as they fled. He glanced back, saw that the other crowd had dispersed. Police revolvers glinted, police whistles rattled their warnings as officers crowded to restore order where fury had struck.

Slipping back, keeping in the shadows, Operator 5 turned darkened eyes on the bodies of two men lying in the gutter. His gaze shifted grimly to another still figure sprawled on the speaker's small platform. It was a ghastly horror in red. Blood marked it with the crimson color of death—and beside the body of the speaker lay the scythe he had held. Torn from his hands in the stampede, its blade had been swung viciously against him; so that now his body, half severed, lay beside the scarlet blade.

Quickly, grimly, Operator 5 hurried from the scene where jungle savagery had overwhelmed sincere intelligence. His lips pressed hard as he hastened past lighted store windows. He paused inside a door and looked back, realizing with a chill that the barbaric power that had struck was a portent of the crisis facing the United States tonight.

HE SIDLED into a telephone booth. The number he called was one known to only a few of the most trusted undercover agents of the United States Intelligence Service. It connected him with the central Intelligence headquarters, WDC-13; and his quick request brought over the line the voice of the chief known only as Z-7.

"Operator 5 reporting," Jimmy Christopher said quickly. In terse detail he narrated the bloody episode in the street, and added briskly: "Chief, I'm positive we're facing a new danger which so far has been keeping itself far beneath the surface. I've been studying the situation for weeks—and now I wish your permission to begin an active investigation."

"You have it, Operator 5!" Z-7 answered tightly. "Please give me your full report as soon as possible. If you believe this incident was deliberately planned and provoked by those men—"

"Men hired—bought killers—using terror as a weapon in the crisis we're facing now, Chief! I'm sure of it!"

"Then go ahead, by all means—in your own way. You must be right—there's some uncanny power at work against us. Only half an hour ago, Senator Grover—leader of the rearmament bloc in Congress—was taking a bill to the White House for the President's signature. The bill is not an important one in itself, but it's the first small step toward strengthening our defenses. As Senator Grover's car turned into the White House, he was shot through the head!"

"Good Lord, Chief!"

"The man who fired escaped. Senator Grover's condition is extremely serious—his life despaired of. If this is a hint of the power which has been acting beneath the surface against us, Operator 5—"

"It is, Chief! Tonight we must face that fact. Tonight I'm sure other steps are being taken against us. I'm going to begin by investigation, Chief, at the Embassy Ball. You'll be able to reach me there shortly—as soon as I've formulated plans."

"Very well—and good luck!" Operator 5 left the phone quickly. Once in the street, he peered toward the spot where death had struck. "Steel means death!" echoed ominously in his mind as his heart quickened with dread. Death! It had been carried to a man advocating national armed strength—and on the blade of a scythe!

THE EMBASSY ball was the gala social event of the nation's Capital. It filled the great International Hall with notables representing all the Powers of a world made restless by threats of impending war. The splendor of military uniforms blended with the color of beautiful women's gowns. The glitter of prized governmental decorations mixed with the sparkle of priceless jewels. A babble of conversations, constant rippling of laughter, subdued the soft music of the orchestra. Here, tonight, nation bantered with nation, belligerents exchanged smiles. The uninitiated might have believed that during these few festive hours all the strife and discord of international enmities were forgotten.

Yet, beneath the laughter and the music, a tide of hatred flowed; a flood of relentless, imperialistic intrigue was rising.

Among the ambassadors and consuls and military officers

waltzing over the glassy floor, a young
man danced with a pretty girl. He was
garbed in impeccable evening-dress,
but wore no decoration of any kind. His
face was clean-cut, his blue eyes strik-
ingly keen; he was obviously American to the core. The gaze of gorgeous
women followed him as he wound his

way through the crowd with his companion. A few of them
noted a strange scar that marked the back of his right hand.

It was a thing of black and white and gray formed, surpris-
ingly, into a spread-winged American eagle.

Every man and women who glanced at him knew instinc-
tively that this young man was one of rare distinction; yet none
of them could dream that he was the ace secret agent of America's undercover system—Operator 5 of the United States Intelligence Service.

Smiling, the very pretty girl with whom he was dancing said
quietly: "Jimmy, what are you looking at?"

"I've been wondering, Di," he answered softly, "at that strange
decoration on the wall. I'd never noticed it before. I'm sure it's
new."

The girl studied the huge mural a moment, while she danced,
before she discovered the emblem which had caught Jimmy
Christopher's attention. It was almost indistinguishable in the
blended colors of the painted scene; yet, once noticed, it stood
out in startling relief. Its strangeness was all the more marked
because it was no part of the decoration,—a long-bladed scythe.

"It *is* strange, Jimmy," Diane Elliot observed. "What does it mean?" She sensed something unusual, something that might make news. As a special correspondent for the far-flung Amalgamated Press Service she had won herself remarkable distinction. In the past, too, she had aided Operator 5 signally in a number of important Intelligence cases; she knew immediately that the omen on the wall bore some secret meaning.

"Strange," he whispered. "There are hints of many strange things here tonight, Di. An unusual under-current, as though something momentous were about to happen. The Capital never stops thinking and talking of affairs of State, but during the past few weeks—"

"What do you mean, Jimmy? What do you think is going to happen?"

"No man can guess," Operator 5 answered quietly, "but it's a certainty that something extremely important is in the mind of every diplomat and military man here tonight. I have an uncanny feeling there's more dangerous spy activity hidden beneath the surface here at this moment than any time since the World War."*

---

* AUTHOR'S NOTE: "The spies of all the nations of the world are up to their necks in work now," is a startling statement made by Captain Henry Landau,

HE BROKE off as an impressive man in perfectly fitting

mining engineer and polyglot adventurer, who was in Holland during the war as head of the 2,000 spies employed by the Military Section of the British Secret Service to gather and transmit intelligence concerning the movements of the German armies.

As an instance, William Burgess, an employee of the Woolwich Arsenal, was arraigned in Bow Street Court in London recently, charged under the Official Secrets Act with obtaining and transmitting to another person "sketches and documents and information calculated to be useful to an enemy" of Great Britain. The nature of the information he was alleged to have communicated or attempted to sell was not disclosed.

The case recalls the sensational affair of the "officer in the Tower," Lieutenant Norman Baillie-Stewart, now serving a five years' sentence on conviction of revealing military information to a German woman whose identity was never learned. Baillie-Stewart was held in the Tower of London for weeks before the nature of his case was revealed. He is now in Wormwood Scrubs prison. A vigorous drive by the German government to stamp out espionage and internal subversive activities was foreshadowed in a semi-official warning against all "sabotagers of the State." The warning followed the imposition of a three-year prison sentence on an unnamed twenty-two year old youth by the dread People's Court. He was said to have served as a go-between in the anti-Nazi "Black Front." The ruthlessness with which the German government is determined to proceed against spies and traitors is indicated by the decree.

So, all over the world, men and women engage in secret work while discovery threatens them constantly with death, and spin a web of intrigue unsuspected by the average citizen whose life and home are imperiled.

uniform touched his arm. Major-General Falk, Chief of Staff of the United States Army and Navy, smiled and bowed. "May I?"

Operator 5 returned the bow as the officer's arm encircled Diane Elliot. General Falk whirled the girl away and Jimmy Christopher left the shining floor quickly. He paused in an archway and again glanced at the huge mural marked strangely—tonight, but never before, he was sure—with the mysterious symbol of the scythe.

About to leave the ballroom, he paused abruptly. A man and a woman, just entering, stopped, facing him. Their eyes were suddenly sharp. Their smiles vanished. Then the features became masks—the woman's an emotionless picture of striking beauty. For only a moment the tension lasted, then the lean man bowed and murmured:

"If monsieur pleases—we may enter?"

Operator 5 bowed. But he did not step aside. "My pardon," he answered suavely. "Forgive me for my rudeness. It is only because I feel that we have met somewhere before, perhaps."

"I am distressed that I do not recall the pleasure," the lean man said suavely. "I am Paul Fiore, attached to the consular service of Urakia. May I present Señorita Rosita Alban, Mr.—" A shadow of a frown darkened his face when Operator 5 deliberately chose not to respond with a name. "I do not remember—"

"It is an error, then," Jimmy Christopher answered, the ghost of a smile on his lips. "I thought, for a moment, that you were Tomas Zastrow, and that the señorita was Mayla Lazare. If I may suggest it—a striking resemblance."

The eyes of M. Fiore sharpened. "Zastrow," he said. "The

14

name is known to me. I have heard him spoken of as—perhaps I do not remember rightly—an international espionage agent."

"Your recollection is quite correct." Operator 5's smile thinned. "Mayla Lazare is a Balkarian, also an international spy—and a very charming one."

M. Fiore laughed—dryly, mirthlessly. "I am beginning to remember that perhaps we have been introduced. Is it not that you are Mr. Christopher—Mr. James Christopher, monsieur?"

The eyes of Operator 5 darkened. "I am sorry our memories confuse us. My name is Walsh—Huntley Walsh." He stepped aside. "My apologies—señorita—monsieur."

They bowed, and passed on. Operator 5 paused beyond the archway to see them dancing slowly on the floor, their eyes searching each other's startledly. His lips tightened again as they became lost in the colorful crowd.

"Tomas Zastrow. Mayla Lazare. Yes, we have met before," he whispered to himself. "And we shall meet again!"

OPERATOR 5 passed a group of uniformed men standing at the head of a broad flight of stairs which led downward. He recognized them as prominent officers of the Joint Board of the Army and Navy—though he himself was unknown to all save a few. As he started down he heard the voice of Captain Jarrell, Representative, War Plans Division, Office of Naval Operations:

"Harreth is coming here tonight. I've just had a telephone call from Bolling Field. He's bringing it with him."

The officer who answered was Major-General Mortman, Deputy Chief of Staff. "Excuse me, gentlemen," he said huskily.

"I feel a little unwell—damnably thirsty for some reason. I've had only coffee, but let me know when Harreth comes and—"

Jimmy Christopher pushed open the swinging doors below as General Mortman started down. He entered the luxuriously appointed foyer of the men's lounge. Immediately a boy in page's uniform stepped close, glancing around cautiously.

"No one else is here, Jimmy. We're alone."

"Good! Keeping your eyes and ears open, Tim? Anything to report?"

"Nothing definite, Jimmy—but there's something strange going on. I can feel it. Do you know what it is, Jimmy? There must be a good reason why you put me on this job tonight—watching the men who come down here."

"There is a reason, Tim—an excellent one."

Operator 5 said no more; the boy asked no further questions. Tim Donovan knew Operator 5 never voiced incomplete theories, spoke when he was sure of his position, never earlier. The tough little Irish lad had executed many instructions from Jimmy Christopher before this without knowing their import, had worked at Operator 5's side through many portentous cases, loyally, courageously. Only his age barred him from the secret roster of U.S. Intelligence agents, yet he had distinguished himself in point of service above many active I-men. A strong bond of affection bound him to Operator 5—a bond which only death would ever break.

"Look!" he exclaimed. "The Postmaster General was down here a little while ago and gave me these!" Proudly the boy removed from a pocket of his page's uniform a sheet of postage stamps. As he displayed them his eyes twinkled brightly in his freckled face.

"See there, Jimmy? They're air-mail stamps, but the plane is upside down. It's an engraver's mistake. The Postmaster General promised me some of these a long time ago. Jimmy, they're worth a lot, and I'm afraid of losing 'em. Will you keep 'em for me tonight?"

"Certainly, Tim." Jimmy Christopher slipped a leather case from a pocket. "They'll be perfectly safe in this." He tucked the stamps into the case, and slipped it through a slit on his hip which vanished as he pulled a thread to close it. "Tim, I've just spotted two of the most dangerous international spies in the world here tonight! It means that something even more important than I suspected is—"

A CHOKING sound startled him. Quickly Operator 5 turned. Fast steps took him to the doors and he pushed them wide. With Tim Donovan at his side, he peered up the stairs at a uniformed man who was slumped against the wall, face contorted with pain—Major-General Mortman, Deputy Chief of Staff.

One hand gripped the chromium rail. The other tore frantically at the stock binding his swollen throat. The veins of his neck stood out in ghastly relief as he began to stumble downward. "Water! For God's sake, give me water!" He groped toward the swinging doors, lurched. Immediately he lost balance and plunged down the steps—spilling loosely until he sprawled and lay still at the feet of Operator 5.

Jimmy Christopher saw the startled eyes of the other officers at the head of the stairs as he slapped the doors shut. He stopped above the fallen man and loosened his stock as Tim Donovan hurried into the lavatory. He was stooping, pressing an ear to Mortman's chest, when the doors banged apart and bewildered officers crowded in. They stopped short as Operator 5 rose, as Tim Donovan rushed back with a brimming tumbler.

"It's too late, Tim," Jimmy Christopher spoke into a tense hush. "He's dead."

Captain Jarrell stared. "Dead? Impossible!"

"Dead," Jimmy Christopher repeated grimly, "and poisoned. General Mortman has been murdered."

The dead man's fellow officers looked at him aghast. He turned briskly, placing his back to the door. His glittering eyes searched their faces. One of them started out, and he stopped that one with a sharp voice.

"Wait!" All eyes turned to him. "Gentlemen, take care. The second most prominent officer of the United States Army has been murdered. Upstairs are hundreds of representatives of foreign governments. It's a certainty that one of them—an accredited agent or spy—is the murderer. Whatever his purpose is, we do not know—but we may be certain that silence will not serve it."

Captain Jarrell demanded raspingly: "What the devil do you mean?"

"General Mortman was killed for an excellent reason, gentlemen—a reason we can't know now. But why was he killed *here?* We can guess at the answer to that. I suspect the murderer wants his death to have some effect on the crowd. Perhaps I'm wrong—

but I urge you to keep it a strict secret among yourselves, at least for tonight, that General Mortman is dead."

One of the officers blurted: "Yes! That is best!"

"Good!" Operator 5's eyes became even sharper. "Gentlemen, do everything possible to remove General Mortman's body without its being seen. Get it out of this building, away from this crowd. There's a rear entrance through the basement, which connects with this lounge—I suggest you use that. Tonight, gentlemen, you'll find it to our national advantage to conduct yourselves with the utmost discretion!"

The officers stared as Operator 5 stepped backward through the swinging doors. His gesture to Tim Donovan warned the boy to remain. Once at the top of the flight, once the resplendent scene of the great Embassy Ball again lay before him, Operator 5 forced himself to appear casual and unruffled. He walked slowly to the edge of the dance floor and his darkened eyes searched the faces of the throng.

Death had struck among them. But they did not suspect— and they must not know.

HE GLIMPSED the thin face of Tomas A Zastrow— the man who claimed to be M. Paul Fiore—dancing with the woman spy Mayla Lazare—she whose secret was hidden behind the false name of Señorita Rosita Alban. Their sharp eyes turned to him. His held; theirs darted away. Smiling grimly, he made way across the floor until he felt a tug at his arm.

Diane Elliot, dancing now with a Major in the Air Corps, whispered to him delightfully. "Jimmy! The Chief of Staff has promised to give me an exclusive interview about strengthening our national defenses. I'm going to make it my biggest story!"

"Go after it, Di," Operator 5 said it quietly, and kept moving. "I think you'll find it highly important." He was aware that she gazed after him in mystification, bewildered by his strange tone. Disregarding, he walked straight to the commanding figure of Major-General Falk, Chief of Staff. Reassuring himself that no one could hear, he whispered:

"General Falk, prepare yourself for shocking news. General Mortman has been poisoned—murdered."

"What! Good God, you can't—"

"Careful, sir! Officers are now removing his body from the men's lounge. I suggest that the matter be kept strictly under cover. Your wishes will decide that, of course, but—there are powerful subversive interests at work here tonight, General Falk. Some diabolical plan is in operation at this moment, and we must not unwittingly further it. These governmental emissaries must not know General Mortman has been cut down by—" Operator 5 was gazing up at the strange device on the mural—"by Death's scythe."

Major-General Falk stood rigid, stunned. Suddenly he strode stiffly away, toward the stairs leading to the men's lounge. Quietly, then, Operator 5 circled the dance floor, toward a corner where men and women were gathered under a balcony.

They were sipping from demitasses, chatting, laughing, while page boys filled other cups from a huge silver urn. Into Operator 5's mind echoed one of the last phrases uttered by the dead man: "I've had only coffee...."

He stopped short near the group when he glimpsed the beautiful Mayla Lazare on the arm of Tomas Zastrow. They were approaching the urn; a page boy was turning a glittering tray toward them. Operator 5's eyes sharpened. He saw Zastrow glance meaningfully at another man then approaching—a prominent American statesman, Randolph Morten, Assistant Secretary of State.

Operator 5's blood went cold. A wordless message had passed between an infamous international spy and an official high in the affairs of the United States!

The realization sent him hurrying toward the corner stairs. He mounted them quickly, moved to the edge of a balcony, and looked down upon the officers and gorgeously gowned women assembled around the steaming urn.

Assistant Secretary Morten had accepted a cup. Zastrow plied gleaming tongs and dropped a sugar cube into that of Mayla Lazare. His suave voice reached Operator 5 above the murmur of the crowd as he inquired of the Assistant Secretary: "Sugar, monsieur?"

"If you please," Morten said.

Again a chill coursed through the veins of Operator 5. He saw the tongs in Zastrow's hand raise again, clawed upon another white cube. It had not come from the bowl. It sparkled unnaturally. It disappeared in the cup held in the hand of Randolph Morten, and the two men bowed.

FOR A moment the international spy and the Assistant Secretary chatted about the ball. Zastrow, the white hand of Mayla Lazare again on his arm, returned to the dance floor. Operator 5 watched the Assistant Secretary drain the demitasse, then glance around furtively. Quickly, unseen by anyone around him, Morten tipped his cup—and a white cube slipped into his hand. It was, apparently, a square of sugar: yet it had not dissolved. Now Morten concealed it in his hand and strode quickly away.

Intently Jimmy Christopher's eyes followed the Assistant Secretary along the edge of the dance floor. Beneath the rail of the balcony, Morten paused, and quick steps took Jimmy Christopher that way. He saw Morten place the fake cube of sugar in his pocket, saw the movement of fingers beneath the fabric of the tailcoat; and deduced that Morten was crushing the impervious shell. His suspicions were verified when the Assistant Secretary's hand reappeared, concealing in the fingers a tightly folded square of paper.

Covertly Morten unfolded it. Operator 5's response was quick. From an inner pocket he brought an eyeglass case. From the case he removed thick-lensed spectacles. He put them on and gazed downward. The specially constructed, powerful lenses acted like strong binoculars. Through them Jimmy Christopher saw a greatly enlarged image of the hand of the Assistant Secretary, cupped about the bit of now unfolded paper. Morten, unobserved, was reading a cryptic message:

Operator 5 tightened as he heard a step nearby. He whisked the spectacles into his pocket, and peered at the man approaching. Immediately his eyes lighted with surprise. Not that the appearance of the man who strode toward him was in any way remarkable—he was wearing the usual tailcoat without any distinguishing decorations. But just as few at the gala Embassy Ball could suspect the true identity of Operator 5, few could know that this man was the commander-in-chief of the United States Intelligence Service. To even his most trusted agents, he was known only by the cryptic designation of Z-7.

Z-7 glanced around sharply. A second man paused at his side—a man also garbed in evening dress, whose face was sharp and chiseled—one of the ablest agents in the service, designated K-2.

Jimmy Christopher heard the chief say softly: "I must see you at once, Operator 5. Please come with me. Attract as little notice as possible."

"Right, Chief." Operator 5, looking down, saw Assistant Secretary Morten shouldering through the crowd at the edge of the thronged dance floor. "May I suggest orders to K-2?"

Z-7 nodded.

"A man by the name of Harreth is coming to the ball tonight on some urgent mission in which General Staff is interested. I want to know when he arrives. Please ask K-2 to watch for him."

Z-7 relayed the instructions to the undercover agent. K-2 turned at once, without speaking, and left the balcony. Operator 5, following Z-7, saw him descending stairs near the great entrance of the International Hall. With the chief, Jimmy Christopher stepped into a small room opening off the balcony. Z-7 twisted the bolt and turned sharp eyes his way.

"I've come here," he declared, "because there's a job of tremendous importance to be done, and because you're the man to undertake it. A task such as we've never tackled before. It's especially dangerous because it involves investigation of a man high in our government."

OPERATOR 5'S eyes widened. "Go on, Chief!"

"Before I give you the detail," Z-7 continued, "I must explain, in all fairness to you, just how dangerous the assignment is. The man who must be investigated is a close friend of the President, and an even closer friend of the Secretary of State. He holds a position which should raise him above suspicion. His reputation is known to every American—a man who is considered high-minded and loyal, who is admired, esteemed. He's also, I'm afraid, a traitor to his country, but anyone who attempts to say so without overwhelming proof is bound to be crushed."

Jimmy Christopher's eyes were a question.

"To make it plain, my boy," Z-7 declared tightly, "you must realize, once and for all, that this task is riskier, as far as you personally are concerned, than any other you have ever undertaken."

"Very good, Chief."

"This man," Z-7 asserted grimly, "has sold out against his government. I've been gathering evidence on the quiet—and I know he's a traitor working secretly with an international spy ring. The welfare of our government demands that we build an absolutely unbeatable case against him—and yet that may not be possible. The country is in a perilous position tonight, Operator 5."

"You may count on me, Chief."

"Good! The man who must be investigated is—"

"Assistant Secretary of State Randolph Morten!"

Z-7 stared aghast. "Yes! But I thought I alone suspected him! How did you know? Never mind answering… you'll take the detail, though you know it may mean complete disaster for you?"

"Chief," Operator 5 said tightly, "I've already accepted the detail. What's more I promise you I'll see it through to the end!"

CHAPTER 2
THE CLOUDING DEATH

OPERATOR 5 glanced past the scores on the balcony to see K-2 returning hurriedly. The sharp-eyed undercover agent's manner was casual as he whispered:

"Harreth's arrived. He's gone into a room downstairs. General Staff is being informed."

"Wait for me there, K-2," Operator 5 directed. "I'll be along in a moment. Do you know an attaché of the Urakian consul who calls himself M. Paul Fiore? If he comes near that room, watch him like a hawk."

Again K-2 drifted away to fulfill orders. Z-7 was studying Operator 5's face intently. Quietly he said: "What's forced a man like Morten to turn traitor is entirely unknown to me, but he has operated carefully. He is absolutely unsuspected, except by me and you."

"Morten may not consider himself traitorous," Operator 5 remarked quietly. "He *might* consider that he's acting in the best interests of his country. He's a rabid pacifist, isn't he?"

"Yes." Z-7's smouldering eyes sharpened. "Is it possible you already have a theory?"

"I can't say now, Chief."

"In any case, no matter what you do, bear in mind, always, that you're handling dynamite. Remember that one slight slip may cost you everything you hold dear. Don't forget that while certain governments cover their propaganda spreaders in this country with diplomatic immunity, the same situation is a thousand times more ticklish in regard to Morten.* You're very valuable to me, my boy—I don't want to lose you."

---

* AUTHOR'S NOTE: The use by foreign powers of members of their Consular service as propaganda and information-gatherers within the United States has been charged by students of international affairs, against the Soviet and Italy.

In 1928 Italy doubled its consular service, the suspected purpose being that there would then be officials enough to carry on both activities. These foreign units of Fascism are controlled, it is said, by Mussolini, who has his men reporting directly to him. It has been charged that the Italian Embassy

"And I," Jimmy Christopher answered seriously, "don't want to be broken, Chief!"

They walked to the entrance of the balcony, and down the stairs. Z-7 whispered "You may reach me at WDC-13 later tonight." He hurried away. Jimmy Christopher spotted K-2 standing near a door, far down a heavily carpeted corridor, and knew that behind it Harreth was hidden. For a moment he stood there, scanning familiar faces in the notable crowd.

Among the uniformed scores he noted those officers who had seen their Assistant Chief dead on the floor. Their ghastly task of spiriting away the body was evidently completed. Now they were striving to join in the banter of those who did not suspect that a human life had been mysteriously taken within these walls. He saw them excuse themselves from their groups and, with strained casualness, approach the door near which K-2 was standing.

Word was being passed through the crowd to the members of the Joint Board, to Cabinet members, to prominent bloc leaders in the Senate and the House of Representatives. Singly and in pairs men disappeared through the door behind which the man

at Washington, and those in Chicago and New York, make their diplomatically immune offices into centers of propaganda and secret nationalistic and party intrigue.

Dino Grandi stated while Secretary of State, under Mussolini. "The consul is the necessary and fundamental element of Italian expansion in the political, economic and cultural fields. The consul is the pioneer in the new civilization which Fascism has established."

Harreth was waiting. Soon the Chief of Staff, his face drawn with the shock of his assistant's death, strode stiffly along the corridor—at the side of Assistant Secretary of State Randolph Morten!

OPERATOR 5 walked briskly forward when the door closed behind the two men. He whispered to K-2 "Keep watching for Fiore!" Then he twisted the knob and stepped through.

Voices ceased as he entered. Every eye turned toward him. The Chief of Staff looked startled a moment, then addressed the others in a low tone.

"Gentlemen, this young man is known to me, and it is my wish that he remain. You may speak with confidence in his presence. I vouch for him absolutely."

Jimmy Christopher noted satisfied nods from those in the room. Among the score of statesmen and officers present were not only the members of the Joint Board but the Secretaries of War and Navy. Several others Operator 5 recognized as famous military men in retirement who now headed national organizations of ex-service men, and patriotic civilian societies. Their eyes turned again toward a man standing at the head of the long table: Harreth.

Behind him the curtains of the huge casement windows had been drawn. A shaded light threw a greenish gleam into his eyes. He was garbed in a wrinkled business suit; he was in need of a shave; he was obviously heavily fatigued. But he was nervously alert. He lowered a briefcase which had been held carefully beneath his arm, unstrapped it, and removed a small cylinder of aluminum. He held it in unsteady hands.

"Gentlemen," he said, "please pardon my appearance. I have been working night and day in the laboratory, realizing the importance of my task. I could not stop when I found myself so near the end of my researches. I have rushed to Washington by plane and asked to see you here because  I wish to put into your hands, as soon as possible—this!" His fingers tightened on the metal tube.

General Falk's voice rumbled. "Mr. Harreth's researches," he explained to the others, "have been known to us for months. We have been waiting for him to perfect his formula. He is placing it at the disposal of the United States government exclusively, like a true patriot. We hope that his success will help to fortify, in some degree, the defenses of this country which have so long and so shamefully been neglected."

"May I ask," Assistant Secretary Morten inquired, "what this mysterious thing is?"

Harreth answered. "It is, gentlemen, an entirely new poison gas. It is called arsenopicrate. It is lethal in very small concentrations. It is a vitally valuable weapon of warfare because no filter now in use can completely neutralize it, and because it defies analysis. If the secret of arsenopicrate is completely guarded by the United States, we shall possess a weapon of war against which no defense is possible."

Randolph Morten blurted: "I flatly opposed the acceptance

JIMMY CHRISTOPHER

of such a weapon! It is inhuman, barbaric, and unthinkable of decent men!"

Harreth paled. "It is my sincere hope," he stated, "that the United States will never be called upon to use this new lethal gas.

I hope that no man ever dies from breathing it. But—however you may protest against it, gentlemen, the fact remains that it exists. I am offering it to this government so that it may never fall into the hands of a ruthless foreign nation. I hope the mere information that the United States possesses such a powerful weapon will discourage all nations from engaging us in a war."

"It is, certainly," General Falk declared, "a weapon of defense, not of attack."

"Exactly." Harreth again fingered the aluminum container thoughtfully. "The characteristics of this gas, gentlemen, are most unusual. Arsenopicrate volatilizes instantly on contact with air, but the viscid fume it forms is extremely heavy. It is invisible, flows like water, and seeks its level. It is ideal for laying down by means of airplanes, but excellent also for spreading from ground stations.

"When sprayed from the air, it transforms itself into a gas while falling. It creates an invisible, lowering cloud of death. When flooded from ground stations, the vapor spreads in an

ever widening pool. In either case it settles heavily and, if it is not disturbed, retains its position until stirred up. Thus, gas may be laid days in advance in territory through which an enemy army is known to be preparing to march. It will lie in wait. When the army moves through, the marching feet and the rolling wheels will stir it up—and spread death. It is the extreme heaviness of the vapor which makes it a unique weapon.

"Also, the vapor, as it becomes diluted with air, undergoes a chemical change. A pungent smell will be noted at first, which soon disappears. The disappearance of the odor—which is itself harmless—will lead the attacked to believe the danger is past. In reality the gas is just beginning to act. When it becomes lethal, it loses its odor. Thus it becomes a doubly effective weapon.

"If this vial were spilled in this room, you would smell the harmless odor and the gas would lie in a pool on the floor until it was stirred up by your movements. That agitation would mean— lightning death."

THE MEN in the room watched in fascination as Harreth unscrewed the top of the metal container. He disclosed cotton padding inside, and from the fluffy tufts lifted a small glass vial. The slender bottle contained an oily, colorless liquid. In silence, Harreth raised it aloft.

"A terrible weapon to be used to enforce peace, gentlemen! Gigantic armament contained in a tiny bottle. I alone know the formula, and I have the only existing copy of it with me. The arsenopicrate in this vial is all there is in the world at this moment. I have brought it here as fast as possible, in order to place it in your safe-keeping. This supply, General Falk, and the formula, I herewith turn over to you, to become, without reserve, the property of the United States."

The Chief of Staff stared at the tiny vial hypnotically as it glittered in the light. "Gentlemen," he declared solemnly, "In almost all respects, the armament of the United States is obsolete and weak. We have fallen far behind in efficiency of defense equipment. Mr. Harreth's work has at last placed in our hands a weapon which is the superior of any similar one in the world. As one who devoutly hopes that the United States will soon properly arm herself, I accept his offer with the deepest gratitude and—"

Even while he spoke, with a suddenness utterly stunning the room was plunged in complete blackness!

No man had moved. Scarcely a breath had been drawn freely while Falk's hand went out toward the shining vial.

Yet somewhere a hand had shot to the light switch and snapped it. A hand, moving so quickly no eye had followed it, had plunged the room into darkness. And suddenly there was turmoil.

"Be careful of the bottle!"

"Let go of my wrist!"

"For God's sake, be careful!"

"Someone's taking the vial!"

"Turn on the lights! Turn on—"

A sharp sound—the splintering of glass—a tinkle of falling fragments. Then silence! Hushed terror.

"The vial's broken!"

"The gas!" choked out of the gloom. "The gas!"

33

Instantly bedlam broke in the room. Men moved panic-stricken through the darkness, driven by a pungency that crept into the air. Chairs fell back. Feet scuffled. Glass crushed again under tramping heels. Men crowded toward the door, choking, gasping, fighting blindly for a knob they could not find.

Operator 5's hand was upon it. At the first clatter of broken glass he had snatched for it. He stood backed to the door in the darkness now, gripping the knob so that it would not turn, shouldering against powerful bodies which crushed against him. He groped toward the electric switch, snapped it. The light threw a greenish glare into horrified eyes. Quickly he twisted against the jamb. His hand, flicking to his armpit and back, brought out a shining automatic.

"The window!" he commanded.

ALREADY CAPTAIN JARRELL had snatched at the catches. He thrust with desperate force against the panes, hidden by the drawn curtains. The windows opened and cold air gushed into the room. Four men leaped toward it while others gripped the edge of the table, sagging down, and while half a score crowded desperately upon Operator 5.

"Let us out!"

"For God's sake, the gas—"

"You'll not go out this door!" Jimmy Christopher snapped. "It would send gas into the ballroom, flow along the floor and kill hundreds. Keep on your feet! Get out the window before it's too late!"

The ring in his voice brought the startling realization home even through their driving terror. They whirled, mobbing across

34

the room, and one by one leaped out, choking, coughing, as Operator 5 sent a swift glance about the floor. He noted the shattered vial, the oily liquid trickling out of it, tracked by quick-moving feet. An iridescent vapor was spreading up from it, torn by the swirling air from the window. The heaviness of the fumes alone had saved those in the room from instant death. Now, because the air was stirring rapidly, death threatened anew.

Two men were sagging to the floor. Operator 5 sprang to Harreth, gripped his arms, dragged him to the window, spilled him out. He heard the door open and close swiftly, but the urgent necessity of assisting the second man kept his eyes from it. Captain Jarrell, eyes streaming tears, helped him lift Rear Admiral Monroe, Chief of Naval Operations, over the sill. As Jarrell sprang through, Operator 5 found himself alone amid the rising viscidity of the vapor.

He sprang toward the door, scraping his shoes on the carpet to free them of any arsenopicrate they might have tracked. He twisted the key in the lock; sprang across the sill and closed the casement windows. Crowding past choking men, he hurried to a rear entrance, stepped into the corridor which led past the room now filled with lethal gas.

Beyond the corridor the orchestra was playing a happy melody; hundreds were dancing, laughter was endless. Again a power of death had struck into the festive hours—and no one must know!

Operator 5 found the corridor empty—until a girl hurried into it from the far end, racing toward him. Puzzled, he hesitated as Diane Elliot touched his arm.

"I've been looking everywhere—Jimmy! What's the matter? You're pale as death!"

"Diane—have you seen K-2? He was here, on orders—"

"I haven't seen him, Jimmy."

"Stay with me, Di! Watch sharp!"

Operator 5 strode toward the archway which opened to the ballroom. As he reached it, a small figure in a page's uniform bounded up the lounge steps. But Tim Donovan's broad smile faded instantly when he glimpsed the grave darkness in Operator 5's eyes.

"Tim, watch that rear door! Look outside it. I want K-2!"

"Sure, Jimmy!"

THE BOY hurried away as Operator 5 stepped into the ballroom. Diane's hand went to his arm. They moved casually, smiling. He paused, gazing again at the great mural in the ballroom, at the mysterious symbol of the scythe.

"Death," he whispered. "It means death... and there *is* death...."

He gazed sharply along the crowd. He was searching for the thin features of one Tomas Zastrow, known as M. Paul Fiore. He looked also for the beguiling beauty of one Mayla Lazare, known as Señorita Rosita Alban. He was sure, when he turned away, that neither of the crafty spies was present.

"Diane, I suggest you find yourself a dancing partner," he said quietly. "I've got a job ahead of me. You can't—"

He broke off as Tim Donovan came hurrying along the corridor. The boy's eyes were wide with dread. He stopped and spoke in a breathless whisper.

"Jimmy! On the court—outside the door—blood! Someone was hurt out there—but there's no one in sight!"

Operator 5's eyes narrowed. He remembered that someone, in defiance of his orders, had opened the room in which invisible death had clouded. The rear corridor entrance offered the nearest means of escape from the building. If K-2 had followed that man out that way—at the thought he put his hand to Tim Donovan's arm as they strode along the corridor.

"Tim, ring the chief at WDC-13. Tell him to send every available man to this building at once. Tell him it must be watched inside and out—or a frightful disaster may occur. Quick!"

As Tim dashed away, toward the telephones in the men's lounge, Operator 5 strode swiftly toward the rear entrance. Diane Elliot paced at his side again. He jerked the door open, peered into the darkness of the open court outside, hesitated, looking concernedly into her eyes.

"Stay back, Di. The devil only knows what force is operating here tonight. You must—"

"It's news, Jimmy—and I'm going to take the chance!"

Operator 5 suppressed a groan. Well he knew the futility of urging caution on Diane Elliot, once she scented a sensational story.

Pressed by the urgency of the moment, he again stepped into the darkness of the court. The music, the laughter of the dancing crowd sounded faintly.

He strode to the corner of the building. Past it he glimpsed uniformed men standing off in the darkness. They were the officers who had fled from the gas-filled room. Several of them were stooping over figures on the grass. Two were carrying another to a waiting car. The rumbling voice of the Chief of Staff reached his ears faintly.

"Thank God, the wind will dissipate the gas leakage before it can do any more damage! Jarrell! Can't you find it, man?"

Operator 5 strode quickly toward the group. He watched another limp man carried to a car, and paused, peering down at a dark figure outlined against the grass, motionless. In the gloom the face of the chemist Harreth was vaguely visible. Captain Jarrell stooped over him and rose with a sigh.

"It's not on him, General Falk!"

THE CHIEF of Staff caught sight of Operator 5. "You find," Jimmy Christopher asked quietly, "that the formula for arsenopicrate is missing?"

"Yes! Harreth said it was the only existing copy. He alone knew it—and it's gone! He alone could reproduce it—and he's dead!"

Operator 5 turned to the man lying motionless on the grass. His eyes darkened ominously as he looked again toward the room which had brought doom to the loyal chemist. He hurried toward the window.

General Falk's voice grated. "This means, then, that the formula is in the hands of a foreign spy, a foreign nation—to be used against us!"

Jimmy Christopher peered through the window. From his waistcoat pocket he brought a small silver case; from the case he removed two oval-shaped wafers of unglazed porcelain. He inserted them into his nostrils—filters, which he had devised in his workshop, capable of nullifying the effects of any known gas. The use of them as an antidote to arsenopicrate was a gamble which might result in instant death. Unhesitantly he opened the windows.

Diane Elliot watched in dismay as he crawled through, closed the casements and crouched to search the floor. Stinging tears came into his eyes as he moved about, breath held, examining every corner. At last, when he was forced to breathe, he sensed a numbing of his lungs—a warning that the porcelain filters were not completely counteracting the invisible poison—that to remain longer would mean his death. Moving quickly, desperately, he readied for a tiny flake of white which lay on the carpet, picked it up.

It bore on one side a fragment of a chemical symbol in ink. As rapidly as possible he continued his search, finding three more such fragments. The blood was pounding in his ears when he reopened the windows and leaped across the sill.

Closing them, he strode into clear air while Diane Elliot anxiously followed, while the Chief of Staff moved to his side. He removed the filters from his nostrils, took a deep breath, studied the bits of paper—and lifted glinting eyes to General Falk's.

"The formula, sir, has been destroyed!"

"What!" Falk barked it. "Destroyed! And Harreth dead! Then that gas cannot be reproduced! It's a lost weapon—a lost defense!"

"It means," Operator 5 said grimly, "that the United States will never use it—but neither will any other nation."

39

He turned briskly, leaving the Chief of Staff started in bewilderment. Diane hurried at his side. He rounded the rear corner of the building and, again in the open court where the music and the lights of the gala ball faintly reflected, began another quick search.

Near the door he paused. His eyes sharpened as he noted dark spots on the cement pavement. His fingers went there, and came away colored with blood. Blood still wet, spilled only a few moments ago. An unknown man had rushed from the poison room: K-2 had trailed him; K-2 had vanished, and now crimson marked the pavement.

OPERATOR 5'S sharp gaze caught other faint red spots beyond. Shifting, he found a trail of crimson circles which led away through the night. Carefully he went their way, toward a high hedge bordering the rear of the court. Diane Elliot was still at his side when he stepped into the deeper gloom behind, when he stopped short, peering at a small enclosed truck which sat a few yards away and almost invisible.

His steps toward it were slow and quiet. At the rear doors of the vehicle he paused and listened. His hand rose to the latch, loosened it. He swung one door wide, peered into the inky darkness inside. A huddled form lay there—white face streaked with blood, eyes closed. He saw that, and no more, when a rush of feet came from behind him.

He whirled at the first sound. Black figures had leaped from the shelter of the hedge—four men. Three sprang upon him, gripping automatics by the barrels. One hurtled toward Diane, stifled her cry of alarm even as she began it.

Operator 5 struck out swiftly, with telling precision, as the three pressed in upon him. He snatched at his own automatic, as a gun-butt slashed hard against his temple. A second clicked viciously upon his head. Brutal, savage, merciless, the onslaught was more than any man could battle.

The lights in the night became a spinning pinwheel as he dropped, unconscious.

IN THE men's lounge of the great International Hall, Tim Donovan wriggled from the telephone booth. He had obeyed orders and reached WDC-13, the central headquarters of the U.S. Intelligence; had relayed Jimmy Christopher's message to the astounded Z-7. Now, anxiously, he bounded up the steps, ran along the corridor, pushed out the rear door into the gloom of the open court.

He caught no glimpse of Jimmy Christopher and his eyes widened with concern. He peered across the lawn where the officers of the General Staff had stood. It was empty now. He searched the darkness as he moved, called: "Jimmy!" He was positive the other had come into this court. But there was no answer.

With quickening heart he hurried into the shadows behind the hedge. The darkness there was as empty as the court. Then his keen eyes detected the marks of tires in the grit. The vehicle which had made them was gone. He was turning to hurry again into the hall when a flicker of white against the ground stopped him.

It proved to be a small oblong of paper, one side white, the other blue, its edges ripped. He peered at it in dismay—and suddenly he burst into a headlong rush which carried him to the rear door of the hall. His small, hard hand closed tightly on the bit of paper as he hastened into the thick of the crowd.

Grimly, anxiously, he shouldered through the dancers, searching for a face he knew. Those he stared at smiled at his evident distress, but there was no smile on his own face. He went on searching desperately—until he saw the man he was hunting. Running to the other he blurted:

"Mr. Postmaster General! Have you—have you given to anyone else here tonight—any of the same stamps you gave me?"

The Postmaster General chuckled. "They're pretty rare, my boy. I venture to say you own the only ones here tonight!"

Tim blurted "Thank you, sir!" He broke into a run that carried him off the dance floor, while scores watched him in amusement. He darted out the rear door, across the court, to the spot behind the hedge. His eyes stinging with the intensity of his gaze, he stumbled along the driveway, scanning the ground. He stopped, picked up bits of white, impatiently tossed them aside, searched farther. It was not until he was beyond the end of the drive that he found a second of the oblongs of blue and white paper.

A sob trembled on his lips as he examined it—an airmail stamp on which the plane was engraved upside down! The stamps he had given Operator 5 for safekeeping! Two, dropped to the ground, had marked the way a car had gone through the darkness. Quickly, eyes sharp, Tim Donovan skirted off along the street, searching anew.

In the great International Hall scores of dignitaries were dancing with beautiful women. Mingling together were ambassadors, consuls, military officers, state officials, matrons, pretty young girls—and spies. Among them death had struck—and they did not know. Above them blazed a symbol of death—the Scythe of the Reaper—and they did not see. These were hours of gaiety and laughter—yet, beneath the surface, flowed a tide of sinister intrigue.

And far out of hearing of the music, along black streets, straining his eyes for another and another of the little blue stamps which marked a dreadful trail, Tim Donovan hastened with pounding heart....

CHAPTER 3
EVIL ALLEGIANCE

THE LIGHT truck swayed along a dark, deserted street. The three men who crowded the driver's seat searched the gloom with glittering eyes, their hands ready on the butts of automatics. Within the latched truck doors, a fourth stood on guard, gun bared, warily watching three bound prisoners.

One lay unconscious, a cruel cut on his temple marked with crusted blood—K-2. The girl in evening dress sat against the side, her slender ankles tied, her wrists pinioned behind her, adhesive plaster strapped across her mouth—Diane Elliot. The third, bound and hunched near the rattling doors, with bowed head, was apparently only half conscious—Jimmy Christopher.

But his helpless posture was a subterfuge, calculated to deceive the guard. The terrific attack had brought swirling blackness to his mind; gradually he had succeeded in clearing his senses. Now, covertly alert, his fingers, unseen by the guard, were closed on the torn sheets of stamps.

The truck swayed as it rounded a corner, and he lurched, tore a stamp from the sheet, thrust it toward the crack at the base of the sagging doors. It whisked out in the draft. A score of times he had done that, the past hour.

Suddenly brakes squealed and the motor hummed lower. He closed moist hands on the remaining stamps to conceal them. Heels gritted at the rear of the truck, and the doors swung open. Two men thrust Operator 5 aside, then climbed in and closed upon the unconscious K-2. They dragged him from the truck, glancing warily around, then lugged him away between them.

The doors closed before Operator 5 could glimpse a single identifying feature of the gloomy street. The men returned to the truck. The latch clicked into place again. The motor hummed. The car started up, and again the armed guard watched Jimmy Christopher alertly.

He deduced immediately that he had been separated from K-2 for some strange, specific purpose. When the truck swerved past another corner he once more lurched against the door, once more sent a tiny square of white and blue into their swirling wake. His sensitive fingers told him that now only a few stamps remained on the sheet, and a cold dread filled him. If they did not last out the journey....

Only two stamps remained when the vehicle, after climbing a short ramp, stopped again. He still pretended semi-consciousness as the doors opened and four men crowded in. Two seized

Diane Elliot, two gripped his own arms. The last stamps dropped unseen from Jimmy Christopher's fingers.

Thrust from the truck, they were forced through the gloom, to a high-hedged yard, and pushed through the rear door of a house.

The guards hustled them through dark rooms. When Operator 5 was—brought to a stop, he felt himself pressed against a smooth, round column. His hands were loosened, drawn behind it, then tied again even more tightly than before. He heard Diane's quick breathing nearby and knew she was being treated likewise. Then the heels of the four men beat away in the darkness. Silence descended about the two prisoners.

THE ADHESIVE plastered across their mouths kept them from conversing. They could only wait during a long, trying interval of uncertainty. Finally, from some room beyond, Operator 5 heard a faint rumble of voices. He recognized the tones of Assistant Secretary Randolph Morten, and his heart went cold. Presently the subdued conversation ceased; an outer door opened and closed. At last, steps came into the room and a sharp metallic click sounded as a light-switch was pressed.

As his vision cleared, Operator 5 found that they had been brought into a deserted house. Evidently a rich home once, it had just as obviously fallen into disrepair. Tar-paper was nailed over the windows; plaster had fallen from the moldered walls; a musty atmosphere filled it. He found that he had been bound to a column at one side of a wide doorway, Diane Elliot to another at the opposite side. Her widened eyes searched his drawn face

45

He tore from the post and with
one swift motion struck away
the fiendish contraption.

now, but he was peering intently at the man who had entered the room.

That man was one who called himself M. Paul Fiore—one who had been known as Thomas Zastrow, international espionage agent.

Zastrow's eyes glittered evilly in his hawk-like face. His smile was thin and ugly. In a low, throaty tone he murmured:

"I have remembered. You are indeed right, monsieur. We have met before, have we not?"

Operator 5 stood straight against the pillar as Zastrow stepped forward. The espionage agent's claw-like fingers gripped the edge of adhesive covering his mouth. With deliberate slowness he ripped it away, and the sharp pain burned Operator 5's nerves. When Zastrow stepped near Diane, and tore the plaster from her mouth with the same slow sadistic pleasure, his eyes blazed with fury.

"Now you may speak," Zastrow declared throatily as he stepped back. "You may cry out, shout for help if you wish, but no one will hear. Allow me to compliment you on your cleverness, Operator 5. Perhaps you find now that you have been too clever—no, monsieur?"

Operator 5 smiled tightly. "I bow to your superior sagacity, Zastrow," he said. "Perhaps, when you are through playing with me, you will explain why you have brought us here."

"But yes!" Zastrow exclaimed. "I am happy to explain, Monsieur Operator 5. I have brought you here to discuss a matter of business. You are a wise young man, and my proposition is one which should interest you."

"You're a bit too sure of yourself, Zastrow," Jimmy Christopher observed quietly. "I'm not in the habit of entertaining business propositions from gentlemen in your profession."

"But you do not know the terms of my bargain!" the suave espionage agent retorted. "It will interest not only you, but the young lady—to a surprising extent, I assure you. It is, I may add, a bargain which gives you a choice between riches and a deplorable death."

"In other words, a plain matter of bribery."

Zastrow's eyes flashed. "Perhaps," he said in a low tone. "Monsieur Operator 5, I do you the honor of considering you our most dangerous enemy. Only your remarkable talents, your privileged position within the United States Intelligence, can be thanked for your being alive at this moment. If you were an ordinary undercover operator, I would kill you here and now and be done with it. But you, monsieur—"

"I will give you your answer before I hear your proposition, Zastrow," Jimmy Christopher interrupted. "It is—no!"

ZASTROW'S THIN smile grew. "You will not accept from us a stipend ten times greater than the wage you are receiving now?"

"The pay I receive for my work is of little importance."

"Even when it involves merely informing us of the moves of your Intelligence against us?"

"You cannot induce me to turn traitor to the Service, Zastrow!"

The spy's smile faded. "Alas!" he sighed mockingly. "Money means nothing. Loyalty means everything. But perhaps,

Monsieur Operator 5, you owe another loyalty even greater than your devotion to the service. Perhaps?"

The ominous tone held Jimmy Christopher silent. He watched as Zastrow turned back to the door, called into an adjoining room. "Brom!" The espionage agent stepped back, eyes glittering.

Through the doorway stepped a short, stocky man. Jimmy Christopher recognized his bestial face immediately. An international espionage agent as dangerous, as ruthless, as Zastrow. Karl Brom, Operator 5 knew, had been enmeshed in political intrigues in Europe which imperiled the peace of the entire world.

The thick lips of the man curved evilly as he drew a stand on rollers into the room. It was a contrivance the like of which Operator 5 had never seen before. It consisted of a small metal tank from which a heavy hose led to a glass bottle. Tubes dipped into the yellowish, viscid content of the bottle, and one of them was bent into a long nozzle. On the tank a clock arrangement was affixed; now it was ticking slowly. While Operator 5's eyes filled with slow dread, Brom wheeled the apparatus to a position directly in front of Diane Elliot.

The evil-faced spy loosened a knurled nut on the standard and raised the nozzle so that it pointed directly at the girl's eyes. He turned a dial at the back of the clock mechanism as Zastrow said throatily: "Ten, Brom. Ten will be quite long enough, I think." Brom turned a brass handle, and a wheezing sound resulted; the rubber hose stiffened. He withdrew, his eyes shining malevolently, as Zastrow came forward.

"A greater loyalty than to your beloved Service—perhaps you owe to this girl, Monsieur Operator 5. She is very pretty indeed, charming, so young! You love her, do you not? Yes! I know! You will see that I am right. Your love for her means far more to you, Monsieur Operator 5, than your devotion to the Intelligence."

Diane Elliot blurted: "That's not true! Nothing you can do to me will make Jimmy betray the Service!"

"We shall see if I speak the truth, mademoiselle," Zastrow answered with a bow. He turned glittering eyes upon Operator 5. "I do not hope now to enlist you to our cause. I expect only that you will give me certain important information tonight—that is all. Do not refuse now, Monsieur Operator 5. You will have ten minutes—*exactly* ten minutes in which to form your decision."

Jimmy Christopher's lips pressed tightly together as Zastrow gestured toward the strange contrivance on the stand. "This device, you see, is a very simple one. In this tank there is only compressed air. This clockwork is arranged merely so that, after a certain lapse of time, a valve will be tripped and the compressed air will rush through this hose. But in this bottle is acid. A powerful acid—sulphuric, to be exact. Ah… I see you understand!"

DIANE ELLIOT'S eyes widened in horror. And Jimmy Christopher tugged vainly, furiously, at his bonds.

"You see," Zastrow said in a purring voice, "the pressure of the air will force a spray of acid out the nozzle. You are of course familiar with the action of sulphuric on organic matter—on human flesh. It will burn deep, it will eat the tissues to the bone, unless the proper counteractive alkali is quickly applied. Reaching the eyes, it will blind instantly. Only a second's application to a skin so soft as this pretty girl's will cause horrible blemishes and scars. You hear the little clock ticking? In ten—perhaps nine minutes now it will release the valve."

Zastrow stepped to the side of the evilly smiling Brom. On the doorsill they paused. Again the master spy spoke in his suave, throaty tones.

"I shall be listening for your call. I leave you to your thoughts, Monsieur Operator 5." The two espionage agents stepped from the room, and the door closed.

Operator 5's eyes turned to those of the terrified girl. Her face was deathly white, her soft lips trembling. Her voice was breathless as she scarcely whispered: "Jimmy, you can't—you can't do as he asks! Don't think of me! Don't—"

"Zastrow's not bluffing about that damnable machine, Di! He's inhuman—merciless. It will work exactly as he says. I *can't* let that happen to you!"

"You mustn't think of me now, Jimmy! The Service—means so much—more—"

She broke off, gazing in fresh horror at the devilish device, at the shining nozzle pointing directly into her eyes. In the bottle the oily, amber acid glittered. A column of it was trembling in the outlet tube, raised by a slight leakage of air past the valve which the clock mechanism would open to the driving pressure from the tank.

The clock mechanism had no face, no hands: it was impossible to guess accurately the length of time already passed, how many minutes remained before the trip would fall. Jimmy Christopher struggled madly to tear his hands from the ropes. The blood throbbed through his swollen wrists, his breath beat hotly with the effort. But the dread truth, that escape was impossible, bore upon him!

He heard the voices of Zastrow and Brom in the adjoining room—and suddenly another sound, slight and furtive, which startled him. It came from the darkness at his back. He twisted and glimpsed a door opening slowly. A gust of damp air came through it, indicating that it connected with a cellar. And in the gloom beyond, a small figure became vaguely visible. Jimmy Christopher's heart gave a great bound, and a name burst in a whisper from his lips:

"Tim! *Tim!*"

IN THE darkness of the cellar way, Tim Donovan stood breathless. With widened eyes he took in the scene. Then, quickly he slipped from the open door, slid along the wall. He peered into the room beyond as Diane turned with hopeful, imploring eyes, as Operator 5 whispered again.

"Careful! They're in the next room! Don't touch that machine—you might trip it! Cut me loose, Tim! Quick!"

The little Irish lad groped in his pocket for a knife. He bared the blade and sawed hard against the hemp strands, listening.

"Gee, Jimmy!" he blurted under his breath. "I wasn't sure! I spotted the truck in the garage and—"

Steps sounded in the adjoining room. "Steady, Tim!" Operator 5 snapped. "Back! Get back! They're coming!"

The sibilant command retreated the alarmed boy into the gloom. He held the knife in his trembling hand and peered at the strands around Operator 5's wrists as the sound of an opening door reached him. He had not had time to sever the ropes; they still bound Jimmy Christopher inescapably.

He heard the purring voice of Zastrow. "Perhaps, Monsieur Operator 5, you have reconsidered? No? There is not much time left, I warn you. Two minutes, that is all."

Operator 5's mind was racing. He twisted, striving to close the space between the column and the jamb with his body. His muscles strained and ached as he tried to cover the gap across which the arm of Tim Donovan must reach to touch knife to rope. The boy, huddled in the gloom, saw the space close. Quickly he stretched, pressed the keen edge again against the binding ropes.

Jimmy Christopher blurted: "I don't trust you, Zastrow! And how do you know I won't lie to you, once I tell you I'll talk!"

"We have arranged precautions against that," Zastrow answered in a low tone. "Your information will be completely verified before you and the girl are released. If you trick us, you will both be punished with the acid-gun. Do not attempt it, I warn you! Now is the time when you must decide, when you must tell the strict truth. Now is your only opportunity to spare this girl life-long disfigurement—and the seconds, my friend, pass quickly!"

Jimmy Christopher felt the knife sawing carefully against the ropes at his wrists. The seconds were passing quickly. His breath caught when he felt looseness at his wrists.

He straightened, eyes darkened, lips thinned. Zastrow's smile was evil, triumphant. The master spy declared throatily: "It is not long now, Monsieur. It is, indeed, less than one minute. It is only a few seconds until—"

Operator 5 snapped: "My answer to you, Zastrow, is exactly as I promised. No!"

WITH ONE swift motion he tore away from the post. His lightning move startled Zastrow and Brom to rigidity as he leaped across the archway. His out-thrust hand struck the glass nozzle and sent the acid-gun spinning on its rollers across the room. He whirled as a cry broke from the lips of Diane; his hand flashed to the buckle of his belt; and at the same instant he heard a sharp, spitting sound behind him.

Oily stuff sprayed from the nozzle of the acid-gun! The valve had tripped. The misty stream shot upon the frame of a window and instantly its powerful corrosive action turned the wood black. Diane Elliot sobbed with hysterical relief; and at that instant the hands of Zastrow and Brom flashed toward their guns.

Operator 5's supple fingers clicked the buckle of his belt loose. He gripped the hilt of a rapier concealed in the long, narrow sheath which encircled his waist. A sharp fling outward of his arm and the flexible scabbard flew from a whipping blade that twinkled in the light. He slashed it downward as automatics flashed in the hands of Zastrow and Brom.

Two shots blasted as he leaped, two bullets puffed plaster from the walls while he struck at the guns with the *épée*.

A howl of rage tore from Zastrow's lips when the razor-sharp blade stroked his hand. His fingers paralyzed, the master spy whirled toward the connecting door. Jimmy Christopher half-spun as Brom's gun spat again and he lunged, his foil flashing, striking sparks on the weapon. Steel clashed steel—as the room was plunged into darkness.

Zastrow had reached the switch near the door; he was leaping through. Operator 5's darting eyes had glimpsed the swift move; had glimpsed Tim Donovan springing forward to release Diane Elliot. Again, in the darkness, the gun in the hand of Brom barked. Jimmy Christopher whirled aside and the blade of his rapier slashed the air as it played upon the spot where the flame had flashed.

Brom moaned with pain as Operator 5 sprang to the dark door. He bounded across the connecting room, snatched at the knob of another door, found it locked. Zastrow had barred the way behind him; the master spy was rushing now to the front of the house. Jimmy Christopher whirled to a window, intending to take a desperate means of heading Zastrow off; but two sharp reports stopped him, and a startled cry whirled him back to the far room.

"Jimmy!"

Operator 5's left hand snapped the light-switch as he sprang across the sill. The glare showed Karl Brom crouched, his gun turned upon Diane Elliot. The girl was not yet free of her bonds. Tim Donovan had been driven aside by slugs slashing through the darkness. Diane was a helpless target before the automatic of Brom—until the sparkling rapier of Operator 5 came into play again.

The keen edge wiped across the hand of Brom. Red gushed upon the spy's numbed fingers. He struck savagely as the gun spilled from his hand. Operator 5 stood rigid, blade poised. "Back!" The command rang from his lips sharply.

Maddened, desperate, Brom struck again—and his motions froze. Face white as death, he peered down at his chest—at a thin strand of steel which his own movement had driven deep into his heart. Operator 5 stood motionless as Brom swayed to the floor. The reddened blade was poised. Quickly, then, he whirled to the column to which Diane was bound. His rapier flicked, parting the last strands at a single lunge. The girl tore away, sobbing with relief, as Jimmy Christopher sped through the arch to the rear of the house.

He snapped back the bolt of the rear door; raced along the driveway toward the street. Bounding past the curb, he peered in both directions, into deep shadows that betrayed no sound or movement. Grimly he stepped back into the gloom as Tim Donovan and Diane Elliot hurried to his side.

Zastrow had escaped. The master spy was gone now in the black maze of the night. Grimly Jimmy Christopher's hand whitened on the hilt of his rapier. He was determined, now, that in the end Zastrow would find escape only in death.

CHAPTER 4
THE POWER COMMANDS

THE CENTRAL headquarters of the United States Intelligence Service, termed WDC-13, is hidden with such canny care that lifelong residents of the nation's Capital cannot suspect its existence. Only a selected few of the undercover agents of the service, through a series of hidden doors and concealed elevator, have access to it. It was here, into the windowless suite of rooms, that Operator 5 came with Tim Donovan, later that same night.

They had hurried together from the house where Zastrow had confronted them; had taken Diane Elliot to her hotel and now Jimmy Christopher was carrying an urgent report for his chief. He strode into an office walled with file cabinets, and paused, peering at a desk beneath a low-hanging light, the top scattered with decoded communications. Keen disappointment shadowed his eyes when he saw that the chair behind it was empty.

The chief dispatched from the adjoining communications room—a clattering, bustling hive to which enciphered reports streamed from sub-headquarters of the Intelligence scattered all over the world, by wire and radio—and placed a yellow flimsy on the littered desk.

"You want to see Z-7, Operator 5?" he inquired. "The chief was called to the White House just a short time ago—direct orders from the President. You'd better wait."

Jimmy Christopher nodded as the communications man withdrew and closed the door. He bent to read several of the topmost reports on Z-7's desk. In one signed with the name of the Chief of Staff, still hot off the wires, he took grim interest:

WDC-13... THREE DEATHS HAVE RESULTED FROM POISON GAS LIBERATED AT CONFERENCE IN INTERNATIONAL HALL TONIGHT... REAR ADMIRAL MONROE CHIEF NAVAL OPERATIONS

HAS SUCCUMBED... RETIRED MAJOR FOLSOM PRESIDENT AMERICAN SECURITY LEAGUE A VICTIM... DEATH OF HARRETH MEANS FORMULA OF NEW LETHAL GAS FOREVER LOST... OTHER MEN STRICKEN BUT RECOVERING... I DEMAND COMPLETEST INVESTIGATION OF THIS DISAS-TER... GENERAL FALK.

"Each of those men, Tim," Jimmy Christopher said quietly, "was working tirelessly in the cause of strengthening our national defenses. They realized completely how weak our armed forces are at this moment and they were doing their best to remedy the condition. Now their support is lost to us."

The Irish lad's eyes widened. "Does that mean it may hold up our rearmament plans, Jimmy? If it does, it's serious!"

"Extremely serious, Tim." Operator 5 gazed at the electric clock on the wall impatiently. "Old-timer, listen. I've got to see Z-7 as soon as possible but there's a valuable lead growing cold. I'd rather put you on that detail than any man in the service. Will you take it?"

"Sure, Jimmy!"

"Good!" Operator 5's hand closed warmly on the boy's shoulder. Turning away, he hesitated, reading another of the most recent reports brought to Z-7's desk. Its import darkened his eyes, brought a new tightness to his lips:

WDC-13... SENATOR GORSON DIED TONIGHT HIS HOME... POISONING SUSPECTED...ONLY SYMPTOM VIOLENT THIRST... DEATH BEING

INVESTIGATED SECRETLY... DMI.

"Another supporter of the rearmament measures—murdered, without a doubt!" Operator 5 exclaimed. "Lord! The secret forces working against us now—!" He peered sharply into Tim Donovan's eager eyes. "Come along, Tim!"

HE STRODE quickly down a corridor lined with doors. One he unlocked with a special key. Its walls were cabinets. He opened several, disclosing military and naval uniforms on hangers, countless types of dress for women as well as men. This was a wardrobe in which there was at least one of every official uniform in the world: here came undercover agents when the necessity of disguise demanded it. Now, from one section, Operator 5 removed the uniform of a telegram messenger, and handed it to the surprised boy.

"Get into this, Tim—quickly!"

"Gee, Jimmy!" Tim spoke as he changed clothes. "You're mighty worried—I can see that. You know you can count on me for any help."

"Tim, old-timer," Jimmy Christopher said solemnly, "until now the country has been under-strength in its defenses due only to the complacency of the people. Now that we are taking active steps to build up the defensive strength we need, there are powerful interests at work—striving to make us remain almost helpless in the face of any other army that might turn against us!* That, and that alone is the reason for—"

---

* AUTHOR'S NOTE: The military forces of the United States rank amazingly low in the scale compared to the military forces of other powers. The follow-

His voice faded off as his thoughts deepened. Quickly Tim Donovan completed buttoning his tunic. At Operator 5's gesture, he followed into Z-7's office—a trim figure in the

ing tabulation of the man-power of twelve great nations, based on figures from the latest authentic available official information, include in each case the active army, the trained reserve, and a separate air force. Military unrest has increased, at least temporarily, the available military man-power of these nations, placing the army of the United States in a still more unfavorable position.

Russia	16,210,000
France	6,952,213
Italy	6,495,535
Spain	2,298,033
Japan	2,177,000
Poland	2,047,035
China	2,004,600
Yugoslavia	1,689,714
Czechoslovakia	1,647,000
Roumania	1,600,827
British Empire	1,141,987
Germany	1,100,500 (estimate)
UNITED STATES	444,661

Amazing these facts are; and it is further true that there are five other nations whose military forces exceed that of the United States—Greece, Switzerland, Sweden, Turkey, and even little Belgium! Moreover, the military force of Portugal, which can scarcely be termed a world power, almost equals that of the United States!

uniform. Jimmy Christopher crossed to a typewriter desk, rolled a telegram blank beneath the platen, and typed rapidly. Tim watched, but only saw meaningless symbols on the page. Quickly Operator 5 sealed the strange dispatch into a yellow envelope.

"It's a fake code, Tim—only a means of getting you into the house." From a metal drawer in one of the cabinets he removed a wedge-shaped bit of hardened rubber. "You know how to make use of that old timer. Now think carefully. When you were following the trail of stamps, did you notice whether you picked one up at the curb of a place at 1300 Avenue Z?"

"I did, Jimmy! I remember!"

Operator 5 slipped another sheet into the typewriter and tapped the keys briefly. He produced the message which he had seen passed to Assistant Secretary Morten by Tomas Zastrow. 1300 Z 12 *instant*. His knuckles rapped the desk.

"Then that's the meaning of the message! Morten received orders to go to 1300 Avenue Z at midnight tonight. It's past midnight now. He may still be there. K-2 must be there too. If he is, Tim, learn as much as you possibly can, and report to me as quickly as possible. You are to try to see Morten there with your own eyes if you can manage it."

"I'll do my best, Jimmy!"

"Good luck, Tim! You can reach me here while I'm waiting for the chief. Go to it!"

Tim Donovan hurried from the chief's office, eyes shining eagerly. Through the secret elevator, past the secret doors he went, until he emerged on the sidewalk of an avenue not far from the Capitol, in front of a cheap restaurant. At the curb several cars were waiting. He knew them to be Intelligence machines, always in readiness. Behind them a bicycle was propped. He mounted it and pedaled off rapidly—for 1300 Avenue Z.

THROUGH INCREASING darkness he wheeled until he neared the address. He left his bicycle at the corner and walked back to an antiquated dwelling occupied, apparently, by a family of no distinction. Shaded lights shone through the windows, and there was a name-plate near the door: *Sebastian Elgar, M.D.*

Tim Donovan's heart thumped as he mounted the steps with the fake message. One hand clutched the stiff rubber device Operator 5 had given him. He touched the bell-button and waited anxiously.

A latch clicked and the door opened; through a narrow crack an eye peered out.

"Telegram," Tim Donovan said. As a hand reached for it he added: "Mr. Kyle live here?"

There was a hesitation, then an impatient: "Yes! Give me the message!"

"I've got to deliver it to Mr. Kyle," the boy insisted. "Nobody else. It's the rule."

"Wait, then."

The eye vanished and the door began to close. Instantly Tim's hand, carrying the rubber device, shot to the socket of the lock. Deftly he inserted the wedge and his hand darted back as the door closed. He stood waiting, suppressing a triumphant smile.

RANDOLPH MORTEN

TOMAS
ZASTROW

KARL
BROM

LEGIONS OF THE DEATH MASTER

BASIL VAN PRAAG

MAYLA
LAZARE

KEEVE

In a moment the door reopened and a man's bearded face looked out.

"I'm Kyle. I'll sign for the message."

Tim passed the envelope and his leather book inward. The man scribbled a name on the page. Without a glance, Tim took the book back, turned, and descended the steps, whistling. The door closed behind him as he strode away.

Once out of sight of the windows, he darted into the shadow of another stoop, and crouched there, carefully watching the windows of 1300.

He saw shadows pass over them, then saw the blinds drawn. He eased back, stood directly beneath one of them, and listened. After a long, soundless interval, he crept up the stone steps to the entrance. Under careful pressure the door opened—the rubber wedge had prevented the bolt from catching in its socket. Tim darted into a dark hallway, and with breath held, stood listening.

From the second floor he heard a voice growl: "The devil! This means nothing! Tell Morten I must see him at once!"

Morten! The name quickened Tim Donovan's breath. He ventured forward, peered into the front room. It was shabbily furnished, glowing pink with the shine of a table lamp. On the table, also, stood a telephone. He took a few steps toward it uncertainly; then, with quick decision, strode forward and lifted it.

In a whisper he asked for the secret number of WDC-13— the number that would open a line for his report to Operator 5.

The voice of the dispatcher at the WDC-13 switchboard

had scarcely answered when a sound in the hallway chilled him. Someone was coming down from the second floor!

Quickly the dismayed boy replaced the telephone and whirled away. The knob of a door in the rear wall drew his hand swiftly. He jerked it open and peered into the darkness of a closet.

Stepping inside, he closed the door gently. The next second heavy steps sounded in the room he had so quickly left—the steps of at least two men. They came close while the Irish lad stopped to peer through the keyhole. He glimpsed shadows as the two men settled into chairs. One was the bearded man who had received the telegram at the door. The other was Assistant Secretary of State Randolph Morten.

MORTEN SPOKE angrily. "I know nothing of this, Keeve! I cannot understand or explain why the message does not respond to any of our code-books."

"You have made a slip! You have placed us under suspicion!"

Morten smiled. "No one will ever suspect me. I have the power to crush and discredit any man in the government who should dare breathe a hint of suspicion against me. I can destroy any member of the Intelligence with a word—even Operator 5. Do not doubt that!"

Keeve impatiently stuffed the telegram into his pocket as Tim Donovan watched. "Very well. Zastrow will see it. I have just had a message from him by phone. He is coming. He's ordered me to learn, from you, why you deliberately destroyed Harreth's formula tonight."

"Need you ask that?" Morten snapped. "I destroyed it because I am determined to destroy the menace of armament!"

"Fool!" Keeve blurted. "That formula was worth millions! You held untold fortunes in your hand tonight and you deliberately threw it away! When Zastrow hears of this he'll—"

"Do not forget," Randolph Morten interrupted in a low, ominous tone, "that I also hold in my hands the power to crush Zastrow if I please—and you, Keeve! Do not forget that!"

The breathless Tim Donovan, peering through the keyhole, saw the two men glaring dangerously at each other. He straightened, his heart hammering. The men in the room gave no indication of intending to leave it soon. The telephone sat on the table almost within the boy's reach—and unreachable. Burning with anxiety, while the voices of the two men resumed, he waited in thick, oppressive darkness.

AT THE desk of Z-7, in the inner office of WDC-13, Operator 5 sat impatiently rereading the reports on the chief's desk. A brisk step in the corridor brought him to his feet. Relief lit his eyes when the door flashed open and Z-7 strode in. The chief's hand sought his as Operator 5 exclaimed:

"Lord, I thought you'd never come, Chief! I have an important report that verifies all our fears concerning Randolph Morten."

Z-7's face darkened. "What is that report?"

Quickly Jimmy Christopher outlined it. He spoke of the suspicious actions of the Assistant Secretary at the Embassy ball, of the message passed in the fake cube of sugar, of Morten's disappearance following the bursting of poison gas in the conference room.

"There's no possible doubt, Chief," he said finally. "Morten's actively working with Zastrow. He's the man who knocked the vial of arsenopicrate from the Chief of Staff's hand—an act that might have resulted in the death of every man in that room. I'm certain that Zastrow, somehow, poisoned Major-General Mortman and that the Assistant Secretary is directly implicated."

Z-7's knuckles rapped the desk. "My boy, I remind you again that Randolph Morten is one of the most highly esteemed men in Washington. I must point out again that he possesses, through his friends and through his office, power enough to break you in a moment. I have come to believe that any attempt on our part to impeach him must end in failure—in disaster for you."

"But I am gathering important evidence, Chief! Tim is following a lead at this very moment which may bring us even more!"

Z-7 DREW a deep breath. "Morten is, as you know, a passionate disarmament advocate. During the World War he lost his wife, his son in active service, his fortune. He's fanatical in his zeal to disarm the world. Yet even those who oppose him on the new rearmament measures respect him highly. I say again that I consider our attempt to prove him a traitor can only end in tragedy for the man who undertakes it."

"I'm willing to run that chance, Chief," Operator 5 declared. "I believe that Morten is dangerous enough—"

Z-7 stopped him with a gesture and leaned earnestly across the desk. "I've just come from a conference with the President and the Secretary of State at the White House. Within the past hour the status of the Intelligence Service has radically changed. We are no longer an independent investigating unit. We are no longer answerable to the President himself. I no longer have a free command of the Service. The highest official of the U.S. Intelligence is now the Secretary of State."

Operator 5 stared astounded. "Chief, that's impossible! It means—"

"It's not only possible, it's a reality at this very moment" Z-7 continued heavily. "The President has ordered me to hold myself responsible to the Secretary of State. The Secretary intends to give orders. What's more he's already giving them—orders which mean hamstringing the Service. He's demanded that I cut down my force by half!"

"What! Why, we have too few operators now for the work facing us, Chief! The Secretary will wreck the service if he—"

"He has the power," the chief declared solemnly, "and he is using it. I pleaded with the President, but it was hopeless. The move's been under consideration for months. The Secretary of State's already been given complete copies of our records, and a full roster of our men. I have here—" the chief drew a thick, folded sheaf from his pocket—"a checked list. Every man whose name is marked is to be discharged from the Intelligence at once."

Stunned, Operator 5 took the roster and peered at it. His extensive experience had brought him into personal contact with every major operative in the Service. He knew scores of them as able, untiring soldiers of secrecy to whom payment for their work meant nothing, to whom service to their nation was an undying devotion. Now he saw checkmarks against the designations of many of the most skilled of them. In bewilderment his

eyes sought the smouldering black ones of Z-7.

"The men oldest in the Service will remain, the newest must be discharged at once, regardless of their abilities," Z-7 declared. "Our secret funds are being cut in half, also, which means that our activities will be drastically restricted." He made a gesture of anger. "This move on the part of the Secretary of State is far more drastic than the abolition of the American Black Chamber after the World War." *

---

* AUTHOR'S NOTE: The American Black Chamber was the name, derived from the similar French *Chambre Noire,* applied during the World War to the Crytographic Bureau of MI-8, or the Military Intelligence Division, No. 8. It functioned with five sub-sections: code and cipher compilation; communications; shorthand or the solution of intercepted shorthand document; secret ink laboratory; code and cipher solution. Its chief was Herbert O. Yardley, who distinguished himself as the outstanding cryptographer of the United States, which distinction he still maintains today, though unofficially. During the World War, the American Black Chamber functioned to intercept and solve countless secret communications, many of a startling nature which have since been revealed, others so momentous in their import that they have never been and will never be disclosed. This work was virtually non-existent before Yardley built up the MI-8 organization. The solving of codes and ciphers had been relegated to the Signal Corps, which, at the time, was working in a hopelessly inadequate fashion. To Yardley goes the

"Good Lord, Chief!" Operator 5 protested. "K-2's name is checked. One of our best men—and even now in the hands of a dangerous espionage ring, a prisoner! That man can't be kicked out of the Service!"

"He will be discharged," Z-7 said with a groan, "because the Secretary of State has ordered it, and there's no appeal from the Secretary's decision. A dozen other restrictions are being clamped down on us immediately, Operator 5. The chief of them is the Code of Intelligence which the Secretary has drawn up. Rules under which we will be obliged to work—as though it is possible for us to carry on our task under a set of rigid regulations!"

DRYLY OPERATOR 5 demanded: "What possible reason can the Secretary have for this action, Chief?"

"A reason which might be considered an excellent one by those not familiar with our work," was the answer. "We, you and I, know that the whole world has a bad case of spy-phobia today. Every nation is hunting hostile spies—and sending their own across the borders of their potential enemies. The United States is under as great a suspicion in this regard as any other major Power. The espionage activities of which the United State

credit for the creation of this vital department of the government; and yet, after hostilities terminated, he was to see it destroyed before his eyes. After sixteen years of ardent work, orders of the then Secretary of State annihilated the Black Chamber.

is suspected may easily, the Secretary of State declares, plunge us into war."*

* AUTHOR'S NOTE: A number of Americans have been apprehended as spies by foreign powers within the past few months. Most notable is the case of two Americans involved in one of the greatest espionage dramas of modern times, who were arrested last year in Paris. The Americans are Robert Gordon Switz, 30, of Orange, N.J., and his 22 year-old wife, Marjorie Louise Tilley Switz, of New York. Mrs. Switz was called by the Sûreté Genérale the greatest spy since Mata Hari. Around the figures of these Americans revolve the whole story of a spy plot which has ramifications all over Europe and in the United States—one so great that its full extent probably never will be known.

Richard Roider, a naturalized American, was held on a charge of high treason in Munich, Germany, recently. He was arrested at Linau last June 22, suspected of attempting to smuggle gold over the border, but this charge was dropped when notes of a political nature were discovered on his person. In Japan, likewise, Americans have been repeatedly arrested, held, and examined by Japanese authorities who suspected them of espionage activities. One recent case concerns a formal request by Japan to the United States to remove the sixteen American language officers attached to the American Embassy at Tokyo from the diplomatic list, which removal would deprive them of diplomatic immunity and make it more difficult for them to enter and reside in Japan. This move is due to recent Japanese charges that a naval language officer in Tokyo had engaged in espionage activities.

The grounding of an American tanker near the great fortress of Tokyo Bay recently led to Japanese naval action to determine whether the crew deliberately beached the vessel to photograph defenses. Naval authorities ordered

73

"But the United States is literally infested with foreign spies—and crippling our service will give them free rein to work against us, Chief!"

"The Secretary of State refuses to consider that a great danger, my boy—though we know very much better. I tried to convince him, but he wouldn't listen. His one aim is to remove the nation from the danger of foreign suspicion, to alleviate foreign hostility by curtailing our espionage work. He'll succeed in his aims no doubt—but at what cost, God knows!"

"At this moment, Chief, the nation is more in need of the full power of our Service than ever before!"

Z-7 sighed, and sank wearily into his chair. "The situation is hopeless. I am now merely an assistant to the Secretary of State, and his orders must stand. My loyalty to my country, my vow to the service, makes that my only possible position. It devolves upon me to execute the orders of the Secretary—and I shall, of course, execute them to the best of my ability."

"I admire you for that, Chief!"

"That's why," Z-7 went on, eyes smouldering once more, "I'm ordering you, now, off the investigation of Randolph Morten."

Operator 5 jerked with astonishment. "Ordering me off? You can't mean that, Chief!"

"If the Secretary of State were not now my superior in command, I would not do so," Z-7 answered. "Since he is, I cannot be guilty of secret insubordination. It would amount to

the tanker, the *Elisabeth Kellogg*, to submit to a rigid examination to check the possibility of the ship's complement being engaged in espionage.

treachery. Somehow—I don't know how—we must get at this thing from another angle. But now your direct investigation of Morten must stop."

"But the power behind Morten is striking at us, Chief! Morten himself is not the commanding mind of this espionage ring. Not even Tomas Zastrow is that. I'm convinced there is a far greater force behind these men—a leader to whom they too are responsible, who gives them orders. If we abandon the Morten investigation now, well be unable to reach that man!"

"The Morten investigation," Z-7 repeated stonily, "must be abandoned now. Let there be no question of that!"

Solemnly Operator 5 asked: "Those are your orders to me, Chief?"

"My orders to you, yes. Operator 5, you mean far too much to the service—I can't risk seeing you broken. You mean far too much to me personally—and I can't stand the chance of seeing your entire life destroyed. That, and the loyalty I can't disavow—compel me to issue those orders."

OPERATOR 5 gazed a silent moment at the haggard eyes of Z-7. "And," he asked quietly, "if I disobey your orders? If I persist in the Morten investigation, regardless?"

"If you do that, Operator 5," Z-7 answered deliberately, "you will oblige *me* to break you."

The tension of that moment was broken by the sudden opening of the door of the communications room. A dispatcher looked in to say briskly:

"Telephone call for Operator 5 on the chief's line. Tim Donovan reporting!"

Jimmy Christopher's hand shot to the instrument. When he pressed the receiver hard to his ear, the whispering voice of the little Irish lad carried over the wire. Quickly, breathlessly, Tim Donovan exclaimed:

"Jimmy! I can't talk long! I'm in 1300—there are men here! They may come back at any minute! I've clinched it, Jimmy! Morten's in the middle of the spy ring, working with Zastrow!"

"Good Lord, Tim!" Jimmy Christopher exclaimed. "Watch out for yourself! You've learned more than I hoped for. Get out there now and—"

"Listen, Jimmy!" the anxious boy interrupted. "In case I can't get out, you've got to get this now! Morten's the man who upset the poison gas and destroyed the formula. I've been hiding in the closet while he talked with a man named Keeve—boasting of his plans. He's sworn to do everything possible to prevent the United States rearming. He's dangerous, Jimmy—and he spoke of discharging you from the Service!"

"Easy, Tim! Try to get back to WDC-13 at once! If they should learn you've got that information—"

"Jimmy, I heard Morten say something about the press associ-

TIM DONOVAN

ation Diane works for—the Amalgamated. He spoke as though somebody big has it under complete control. He—"

Abruptly Tim Donovan's voice rose to a frantic cry. Jimmy Christopher tightened as he heard a growling voice behind the boy's. A sharp clatter came over the line, the distant telephone falling. The crack of a violent blow followed, and a moan of agony. Motionless, breath stopped, Jimmy Christopher heard Tim Donovan's voice groan his name.

"Jimmy!… Jimmy!…" Then a click—and the connection was broken.

Operator 5 lowered his instrument. During a moment of mental turmoil he peered at Z-7; and the chief said quietly:

"Hold yourself ready for other orders, Operator 5. So far as you, and the entire Service is concerned, the Morten investigation is ended."

Words crowded to Operator 5's lips. "So far as I'm concerned, Chief, the Morten investigation has just begun!" he wanted to say.

He pressed the bitter statement back. Without speaking, his eyes glittering dangerously, he turned on his heel. Z-7 peered after him in amazement as he strode out of the inner office—hurrying along the secret way that would lead him from WDC-13 into a world threatened with an unknown intrigue of vast and startling ramifications.

CHAPTER 5
THE SUPREME ULTIMATUM

O PERATOR 5 grimly took the wheel of his stream-lined roadster, at the curb in front of the hidden central headquarters. Still clad in the expertly tailored evening suit, his silk hat tilted at a jaunty angle, he raced the car away from the buzzing hub of the Capitol. The warning orders of the Washington chief still rang mockingly in his ears.

Presently he swerved to a curb. From the wheel he peered at the gilt number of the house before which he had stopped:

1300. His gaze went from window to window, and he listened. As a plan formed in his mind—a plan which, because of Z-7's orders, he had to execute single-handed—he reached to the door of a metal cabinet bracketed beneath the dash. When he left the roadster he was carrying three strange objects in his gloved hands.

Moving silently to the windows, he reached to the sill of the first and left there an oblong article the size of an octavo book. At the second sill he left a similar device. The third item—a black, square box—he carried with him as he unhesitantly trod up the stoop to the door.

He turned a winding-key affixed to the black box, raised it to the upper, inner corner of the entrance and pressed it hard to the wood. He turned two wing-screws, and sharp threads bit deeply, holding the device in place. His preparations completed, and his eyes glittering darkly, he touched the bell-button.

While he waited, his hand slipped beneath his coat to his arm-pitted automatic. Soon quick steps approached; the door opened in response to his summons. In the gloom a single eye peered out at him. He rested his mocha-gloved hands on his silver-capped stick and spoke quietly.

"Good evening. Two friends of mine, I believe, are here. I wish to see them."

"Friends—of yours?" a husky voice asked in surprise through the crack. "There is some mistake. I do not know you."

"There is no mistake," Jimmy Christopher answered firmly. "The name of one of my friends I cannot give you, but the name of the other is Tim Donovan. He is a young chap, wearing the uniform of a messenger boy—a disguise, of course, as you know."

A startled gasp answered Operator 5's daring statement. Instantly the door began to close. Jimmy Christopher's stick flipped swiftly into the crack. Briskly he stepped forward, came to an erect standstill in the hallway as the door closed behind him, and peered at the astounded, bearded face of the man who had attempted to keep him out

"Thank you very much," Operator 5 said with a biting ring in his voice, "for inviting me in. My friends are not expecting me, but I believe they will welcome my call."

The bearded man blurted: "Who the devil are you?"

"Please pardon me if I withhold my name," Jimmy Christopher answered with a tight smile, "but perhaps it will suffice if I say that I am a member of the United States Intelligence. You, I believe, are one Peter Keeve, espionage agent-at-large—a gentleman I should not care to turn my back upon."

THE HEAVY brows of Keeve lowered ominously. The glitter of his shaded eyes testified to the racing of his mind. He forced a hard smile, and attempted to equal the suave daring of Operator 5's manner—attempted it unsuccessfully.

"Quite so," he said. "At first I did not understand. Your friends are here. They are not exactly prepared to receive company, but—shall I take you to them?"

"If you please," Operator 5 bowed.

Keeve turned promptly, and began to climb the stairs. Operator 5 followed with brisk step. He noted, in the gloom of the landing, startled eyes peering down at him. A guttural command from Keeve sent those who were watching into swift retreat. When Operator 5 reached the landing, the hallway was empty. He turned with Keeve—and stopped short.

Through the door they were approaching a hoarse scream sounded—the cry of a man in agony. It trembled away to a moan while Operator 5 stood motionless, his blood running cold. Silence returned. Keeve's heavily shadowed eyes glittered evilly.

"That was a hearty laugh, was it not?" he asked throatily. "One of your friends is enjoying himself greatly. You will join him?"

The chubby hand of Keeve twisted the knob. Bright light streamed outward silhouetting the gorilla figure of the spy. He stepped through quickly, uttered another guttural command; and Jimmy Christopher followed with quick stride. He paused just inside the door as Keeve closed it behind him and his face went hard.

The two men who had whirled to face him glared malevolently. Operator 5 had never seen their repulsive faces before, but from photographs on file at WDC-13 he recognized them. Stahr, and Radak, both notorious spies whose allegiance was for sale to any nation willing to pay the price of their services. Operator 5 gave them only a glance; his gaze turned quickly to a cot at the side of the room.

Tim Donovan was lying on it, his hands and ankles bound by twisted wire, a gag fastened into his mouth. His eyes widened in terror, flashing a warning to Jimmy Christopher, as he strained up. Suddenly Radak turned and struck at the Irish lad savagely. His flat palm slapped sharply across Tim's face, and the boy fell back, stunned, Operator 5 held himself back as a moan came

from Tim's throat; and his eyes grew ominously black—black as the darkness of the night which shrouded this remote house.

Nor did he speak when his gaze turned to the second of the prisoners held within this room. Bound to iron rings set in the

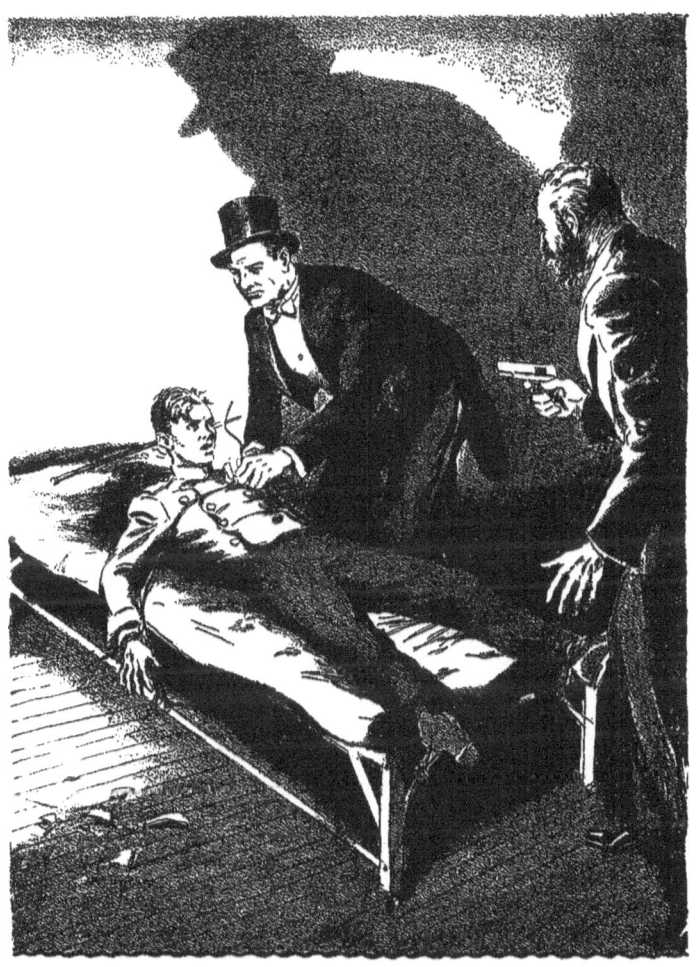

Jimmy Christopher saw the three muzzles looking at him like dead eyes!

wall, hanging to them exhaustedly, the scalp near his temple torn by a cruel blow which had left a brown-crusted cut, was the U.S.I. man known as K-2. His face was drawn and as pale as death. His gaze implored Operator 5.

Around his neck a noose of thin wire was circled. By means of a wooden handle the strand had been tightened until now the flesh bulged over it and red trickled downward from the cuts it had caused. It was another twist at the noose that had wrung from K-2's lips the strangling cry which Operator 5 had heard in the hallway. Now Radak and Stahr stood at the sides of the panting K-2, their hands stealing toward their guns.

OPERATOR 5 stood motionless, while the bearded Keeve said gutturally: "We have been amusing our guest with a little game. He endeavors to remain silent while we endeavor to induce him to utter a few words we want to hear. I rather think that at present the odds are in our favor."

Jimmy Christopher stated briskly: "Your game is at an end, I assure you. It is, shall we say, a draw? Please release this man and boy immediately."

Keeve turned to face Operator 5. "We are inclined to continue amusing ourselves. You will, perhaps, care to take part? You will find yourself greatly entertained."

Operator 5's glance turned again to Stahr and Radak. Now their guns had left their pockets. Now two automatics were leveling at him. A quick motion on the part of Keeve brought a third ugly weapon into the light. Jimmy Christopher saw the three circles of the muzzles looking at him like dead eyes.

"You have been, if I may suggest it," Keeve muttered, "rather foolhardy to come here alone!"

Operator 5 forced a smile. "Do you imagine," he asked, "that I have come alone?"

The eyes of the three men flickered. They searched the calm face of Operator 5.

With the greatest of assurance, he stepped past Radak to the cot. While the men stared he stooped and unwound the wires which bound Tim Donovan. He turned back as the breathless boy scrambled up, and again he smiled.

"You might," he said, "succeed in killing me here in this room, it is true. Whether or not you choose to attempt it is strictly up to you, gentlemen. I should not advise it. It might be equivalent to committing suicide on the spot."

Fear shone in the eyes of the three men as Operator 5 stepped to K-2. Again he twisted loops of wire. The exhausted undercover agent breathed in torturous gulps as the noose came free of his throat, as his hands and ankles were detached from the rings. He sagged against the wall, his haggard gaze upon the cool one of his rescuer.

"Those who kill members of the Intelligence are handled, shall I say, rather roughly by the Service," he said levelly. "Perhaps you would like, as much as I and my friends, to leave this house alive. If so, I urge decorum upon you, gentlemen. We're going now. Do not, I warn you, attempt to stop us."

Deliberately, his confident manner still bewildering the three, he opened the door. He signaled the amazed Tim Donovan and K-2 through. Just as they started for the stairs, Keeve bolted out.

"It's a bluff!" he snapped. "He's alone! He's got no one behind him! Look out the doors, Stahr! Make sure this house is not surrounded and then—"

At the door below sounded a sharp rapping! Loudly, insistently the sound echoed from the front entrance. Stahr had started to crowd past Operator 5; the knock stopped him short. Radak had begun a run toward the rear stairway and the tattoo brought him to a cold standstill.

From Keeve's thick lips another warning burst: "They're at the front door!"

AGAIN THE sharp rap sounded; and Operator 5 bounded down. "Quick!" he ordered Tim Donovan and K-2. From the landing above came the sounds of quick-moving feet as doors opened, as unseen men crowded out of the closed rooms. He sped to the lower hallway as Keeve shouted again from above:

"Out the back! Shoot down anybody who tries to stop you! Don't let them get away! Don't—!"

An automatic blasted at the top of the stairs. The bullets slapped into the jamb of the front entrance as Operator 5 reached for the knob. Instantly he whirled, his gun flashed from armpit to gloved hand. Twice, swiftly, he sent slugs whistling upward. Keeve's second bullet crashed as Jimmy Christopher snapped the door open. Past him crowded the breathless boy and the dazed K-2, as his gun lashed lead again. And while he darted out, the knock sounded again—a knock made on the door by no human hand!

Inside the little black box which Operator 5 had screwed to the door a hammer was working, driven by a coiled spring through a mechanism, simulating the sound of someone demanding entrance!

Keeve roared. "It's a trick!" His snarling voice promised death to Jimmy Christopher as the door swung shut. Quickly Operator 5 slipped a small metallic L-shaped device from his pocket. He pressed the shorter, sharp-edged angle into the wood as a bullet drilled through near his head, pulled the door shut, and the longer angle protruded outward. Through a hole in it he slipped a short steel rod also whisked from his pocket. Immediately the knob twisted as someone pulled at it. But the device held.

Tim Donovan and K-2 stumbled into the roadster as Jimmy Christopher sprang to its far side. From inside the entrance Keeve snarled, "Get them through the windows!"

Jimmy Christopher's automatic leveled as dark, flickering motions showed behind the front panes. Twice he fired, swiftly, tellingly. One bullet sped to the book-shaped device he had left on one of the sills; his other streaked to the second. Instantly both crashed to bits; instantly flame sprang upward. Acid, spattering from one compartment of each device, had mixed with a flying explosive powder.

Howls of rage sounded within the room as the roaring burst of flame forced the men in there back. Through the billowing flames and the black smoke bullets snapped as they fired wildly. Operator 5, slipping behind the wheel, answered the shots as he threw his machine into gear.

Once the flames whipped away to expose broken panes— and a face peering outward, dark-lined in the glare. It registered unforgettably on his mind as he roared away from the curb—the face of Assistant Secretary of State Randolph Morten!

The car spurted along the empty street, swung swiftly around the next corner. Tim Donovan exclaimed, "Gee, Jimmy... ten men in there—and you got us out single-handed!"

Operator 5 scarcely heard. He pressed the motor to the limit when he twisted the wheel again—and sped, his face grim, toward the center of the nation's Capital.

Z-7 SAT at his littered desk in the inner office of WDC-13, peering at an imposing typewritten document. It was headed *Code of Intelligence*. It was couched in hard, stern terms and its last page bore the signature of the Secretary of State. Z-7's jaw-muscles lumped with anger as he read the numbered paragraphs; but he came to his feet with alacrity when the door opened and Operator 5 strode in.

Following Jimmy Christopher came K-2 and Tim Donovan. The secret agent was weak from the blow and the torture he had suffered. The Irish lad's eyes sparkled in alarm. Z-7 studied their faces in amazement and demanded: "For God's sake, what does this mean?"

Quietly Operator 5 said: "Chief, before I left here a short while ago, you ordered me off the Morten investigation. I want to know, here and now, if those orders still stand."

"They do, Operator 5, absolutely!"

"If," Jimmy Christopher persisted, "I take any action against Morten, directly or indirectly, you will consider me guilty of insubordination?"

"I will be obliged to do that, yes!"

"I understand that clearly, then, Chief." Operator 5 peered grimly at Z-7. "K-2 was injured at International Hall tonight, but he does not know who attacked him. Tim telephoned me an alarm a short time ago which has come to nothing. That must comprise my report now, Chief."

Z-7's eyes smoldered. His stubby fingertips rippled on the desk as he studied Operator 5's determined face uncertainly. Suddenly, thrusting suspicions aside, he took up the Code of Intelligence and proffered it to Jimmy Christopher.

"There are the rules and regulations under which the Secretary of State expects us to work," he stated. "Read them carefully. The Secretary will enforce them to the letter and break any man who disobeys them."

Operator 5 peered at the formidable document, and sank into a chair. Tim Donovan leaned to read with him. K-2, sighing with pain, paused when a low word from Z-7 addressed him. The Washington chief reached for one of a stack of orders-forms on his desk. They were dispatches ready to be sent to every Intelligence operator whom the Secretary of State had selected for discharge from the Service. The one which Z-7 held now was addressed to K-2.

"This—this is a damned hard thing to do," he began bitterly. "You're one of our best men, K-2. I can only say that this reflects in no way on your service in the past. But it's—final."

K-2 peered at the orders, stunned. His bleared eyes glimpsed phrases.... "Pursuant to orders of the Secretary of State... discharge from the service effective at once... personal gratitude... regrets." Unbelievingly, the undercover agent stared at the slip of paper which completely severed his connection with the Intelligence. Then he swayed as if struck.

"I don't understand, Chief!"

"I'm sorry, K-2," Z-7 said sincerely. "I'm sorry as the devil."

"I'm out—of the service—for good and all?"

"Yes."

THE STRICKEN man sank into a chair. Clearly the hurt that filled him was a keener pain than the wound on his head, the lacerations on his tortured throat. Appalled, paralyzed, he peered at the yellow sheet of doom. He was unaware that Operator 5's eyes were upon him, and burning with deeply felt sympathy. Jimmy Christopher realized that a sentence of death could have been no heavier a blow on K-2. Grimly he rose and tossed the Code of Intelligence to the chief's desk.

"It's impossible for us to work under those regulations, Chief! Section 23 hog-ties us! I would rather quit the Service than attempt to work under it!"

Z-7 sprang up in dismay. "My boy, don't say that! Listen to me. I regret this as deeply as you, but I can do nothing to change the Secretary's decision. I want you to remain in the Service, no matter what happens. I implore you, never to quit the Intelligence as long as I am chief!"

The earnest ring of that voice brought warmth to the heart of Operator 5. His eyes softened. He extended his hand, gripped Z-7's.

"You're right. Chief. We've got to carry on the Intelligence as best we can, no matter what handicaps are forced upon us. As long as you're my chief, I'm going to stick, and I'll be proud to work under your orders."

"Thank you for that, Operator 5!"

"But I can't supinely accept that code!" Jimmy Christopher protested. "The situation we're in now absolutely demands that we do everything possible to strike it out. May I see the Secretary of State about it? Can you arrange it, Chief—tonight?"

"I'll try."

While Z-7 called the office of the State Department, Operator 5 reread the drastic Section 23 of the iron-bound code. It read tersely:

> 23. No investigation of any alleged espionage activity by any foreign nation may be undertaken by the Intelligence or by any civilian without a full report of the circumstances having been first filed with the Secretary of State, nor without his specific approval that the investigation may proceed.
>
> The penalty for disobedience of his clause by a member of the Intelligence is instant dismissal.
>
> The penalty for disobedience by a civilian is imprisonment in a federal penitentiary for not less than ten years nor more than one hundred.

"It means dishonor for any man of us who serves his country in spite of the Secretary's code, Tim!" Operator 5 exclaimed. "It may mean life imprisonment for anyone outside the Service! A horrible price to pay for loyalty reaching above hide-bound rules!"

Z-7 turned briskly from the telephone. "The Secretary is still in his office, Operator 5. He will see us at once. He's warned me that this will be our only opportunity to protest any of the sections of the new articles."

"Please come with me, Chief," Operator 5 asked tightly as he rose. "If it means that we've got to fight it out with the Secretary tonight, we'll fight it our best! The whole future of the Intelligence—the very destiny of the United States—depends on it!"

CHAPTER 6
REPORT AND CHALLENGE

O PERATOR 5 stood at the side of Z-7 in the Secretary of State's private outer office in the great State, War and Navy Building, just west of the White House on Pennsylvania Avenue. Beyond a door rumbled weighty voices. The two Intelligence men paused impatiently until it opened and a man stepped out.

At sight of him, Operator 5's lips tightened.

It was the face he had last seen, lined with grim fear, behind the sheeting flames of the windows of the house at 1300 Avenue Z. The face of Assistant Secretary of State, Randolph Morten!

"The Secretary," Morten said huskily, "will see you gentlemen now."

Amazement at the cool daring of the man filled Operator 5 as he stepped inside. Morten followed Z-7 into the room and stood beside the door. Jimmy Christopher gripped the Secretary's hand.

"I will listen, of course, to your recommendations," that dignitary declared, "but I am obliged to warn you that the Code of Intelligence will be enforced as it stands."

Operator 5 stiffened. "Mr. Secretary," he said, "you are aware that there are hundreds of foreign espionage agents operating within the United States."

"I am also aware," the Secretary stated, "that to act unwisely against any foreign nation on that basis may result in a grave international breach which might lead to war."

"You are also aware," Jimmy Christopher continued, "that in certain cases, espionage activities have reached ominous proportions—especially on our west coast?"

"In the specific case you refer to," the Secretary answered, "we must be especially careful not to over-strain our international relationship."

Operator 5 glanced again at Randolph Morten, who was still standing near the door listening. "Forgive me," he said quietly. "May the chief and I speak with you alone?"

The Secretary's eyes grew cold. "Young man," came the frosty answer, "before any member of my staff you may speak as freely as though to me alone. I resent your implication that you may not. If you wish to consult with me tonight concerning the code—and this is your last opportunity—please proceed directly."

Jimmy Christopher's face flushed. "I have asked to see you alone," he persisted, "because the most vital case before the Intelligence now suggests that there is treason within your Department, sir!"

Z-7 paled. The Secretary's hands curled into huge fists. He glared across the desk and blurted:

"What! You dare to suggest that any of my staff is traitorous? Young man, every man in this department is my personal friend. I will not tolerate any such innuendo from anyone! I consider it an insult—and I consider this interview terminated here and now. Good night!"

Operator 5 did not move. His darkened eyes battled the Secretary's. Then he leaned forward tensely, placing his hands flat on the desk. His words rang.

"Mr. Secretary, my only purpose, and your only purpose, is to serve our country to the best of our abilities. The means we would take are in violent conflict, but on that basis at least permit me to express my views. If you will allow me, I will explain."

The Secretary stared stonily and said nothing.

Jimmy Christopher continued briskly, "The United States is at present undertaking a vast program to strengthen our defenses. The necessary legislation, calling for the needed appropriations, is soon to go before Congress. The decision of Congress on these matters will be final—and vital. The nation is torn tonight between two great factions—one preaching disarmament, the other pleading for strengthened defenses.

"Both sides of the issue are doing everything possible to bring the mass of the people behind them, in order to influence Congress to their way of thinking. Personally, I stand behind the rearmament forces, but my position is of no importance. My concern in this case is that there are subversive powers plotting to keep the United States weak and helpless among the great Powers of the world. A great spy ring is in operation, stopping at nothing to disrupt the rearmament move. Already they have killed noted leaders of the rearmament cause. They have committed sabotage upon our statesmen just as certain foreign nations are believed to have committed sabotage upon our present weak war equipment!" *

"Absurd!"

"You do not realize, Mr. Secretary," Jimmy Christopher persisted, "how deeply this secret organization is at work, how

---

* AUTHOR'S NOTE: Sabotage, linked with the presence of Filipino mess boys aboard U.S. Navy airships, was suggested recently to a House committee taking evidence in the loss of the *Macon* and *Akron*.

Roy W. Knabenshue, pioneer dirigible designer, told the House Patents Committee: "If an investigation could be made of the structure and wreckage, I believe it would be found that sabotage had something to do with the destruction of the *Macon*."

Knabenshue said he did not believe the airship officers had any connection with possible sabotage. Chairman Sirovich asked if he thought any foreign governments might have had anything to do with it.

Knabenshue replied: "I'd hate to say."

Later when asked if the mess boys might have been employed by the Japanese, he replied: "It is possible." He pointed out only two of the *Macon's* crew perished and one of them was a Filipino. He said on further questioning: "Yes, the Filipinos are fatalists.

"If divers can bring up the wreckage, I believe they could establish that sabotage had something to do with the failure of the *Macon's* steering fin.

"Such sabotage might have occurred while the ship was in flight."

mercilessly it has already struck at the heart of our rearmament program. Tonight Major-General Mortman was murdered by one of that secret ring. On the chief's desk now is a report which means that Senator Gorson was murdered in the same way by the same organization. Tonight a man in the employ of the master spy destroyed, beyond all reclaim, a new weapon of war which would have given the United States terrific power."

Jimmy Christopher sensed an electrical tension in Randolph Morten; but his eyes did not leave the stern face of the Secretary.

"That's only a suggestion of how the ring is working!" he declared. From his pocket he removed a folded sheaf of yellow flimsies. "These are copies of reports recently received at WDC-13. Each one indicates the operations of the great spy ring. Look at them, Mr. Secretary.

See how the secret band is working night and day, mercilessly, in order to keep the United States a weak and defenseless nation!"

He tossed the reports to the Secretary's desk and raced on. "There you will find records of other mysterious deaths—each victim a man who was striving to uphold our rearmament program. There you will find cases of men who once gave the movement their support, who have about-faced and are now campaigning against it—men who have sold out. Major-General Clayson, retired, one of the defense program's staunchest supporters, vanished a month ago—again the work of the spies! Other armament men have left the country, not to return—driven away by threats of the spies.

"Why have these things happened, Mr. Secretary? Why have

the leaders of the organizations backing the defense programs suddenly found it necessary to provide themselves with bodyguards? Why have speakers in favor of the new program abruptly canceled their arrangements? Why have great broadcasting chains gone mysteriously out of operation during the speeches of Army officers talking in favor of strengthened defenses? Why are there propagandists arousing the people against the program—propagandists who can't be identified or traced? The answer is—a gigantic espionage ring laboring to keep the United States so weak it will be a helpless prey before any attack!"

THE SECRETARY snorted: "Preposterous!"

"But it is not preposterous to say—because it is true—that the United States is in a gravely perilous position today. Not only are we unarmed, but we are forced to rely on foreign nations for almost all our war materials.* The situation is one, sir, that will some day mean the extinction of this nation unless it is corrected. The spy ring is working desperately to make it possi-

---

* Author's Note: Rear Admiral Yates Stirling, Jr., Commandant Brooklyn Navy Yard, formerly Commander of Naval Station, Pearl Harbor, Hawaii, graphically pointed out recently the dependence of the United States upon foreign markets for materials of defense. "Foreign naval strategists glibly tell us," he said, "that the United States is, for all practical purposes, self-contained and could subsist in time of war on its natural resources. In times past, this might have been true, but it is not true today, nor will it ever be again.

"The vast industrial organization of the United States today is vitally concerned in the continuous supply of raw materials, most of them coming

ble for any foreign nation to wipe us off the face of the earth whenever that nation chooses!

by sea from foreign territories. Many of the articles are vital to the preparedness of the nation for war.

"In the year 1926, one of our prosperous years, the United States imported raw materials to the total value of two and a quarter billion dollars.

"Without these imports, the Department of Commerce informs us, we would have been deprived of foods essential to our well-being; metals necessary to support our industrial civilization; chemicals and drugs upon which medical science rests, and raw products without which many of our factories would close and our labor population suffer privation if not starvation.

"The people of the United States in 1925 had invested ten and a half billion dollars abroad in copper, tin and iron ore mines, in paper and pulp mills, in petroleum, silver, asbestos, manganese and rubber. The importance to our industries of these imported raw materials, together with our investments abroad, has given over a hostage into the hands of those nations who may for their own ends desire to harm us by a ruthless control of the seas in diverse areas in peace or war; an added reason for the maintenance of all our elements of sea power.

"The people of our country have been late realizing and acting upon the now evident fact that sea power is a vital handmaiden of our national prosperity. The natural consequence has been the lack of adequate sea power, almost since the beginning of our history as a nation."

The mission of our sea power is defensive, but the instruments are designed throughout for offensive action. Rear Admiral Stirling concluded his outline of this startling situation with a plea that our position absolutely demands a greatly strengthened navy.

"Whether or not the United States rearms now," the Secretary declared, "depends wholly upon the will of the people."

"It *should* depend on the will of the people, but unless we act and act promptly, it will depend instead on the will of the unknown man who is the head of this espionage ring—and we will be doomed!"

The Secretary's eyes snapped. "And what," he asked coldly, "is it you wish? To proceed upon this ridiculous theory and incur the enmity of every other nation on the globe? To risk plunging us into war when we are still unprepared? Have you forgotten, young man, that the Department of State is this government's Department of Peace?"

"I wish, sir," Operator 5 answered levelly, "to be allowed to follow this case through, to try to destroy that espionage ring."

"Under Section 23 of the new Code of Intelligence, you absolutely must have my permission for that, Operator 5."

"I cannot even ask your permission, under these certain circumstances, sir. I ask that Section 23 be struck out of the code so that I may go ahead unhampered."

"These certain circumstances you speak of," the Secretary asked icily, "are your belief that someone in this Department is involved in your so-called espionage ring."

Operator 5's face whitened as he answered: "Yes, sir."

The Secretary snapped. "I refuse to credit that belief for one single moment! Section 23 must stand! As for permission for you to continue, I refuse it absolutely."

Operator 5 stood motionless, tense, his darkened eyes upon the Secretary's. "That, sir," he asked, "is final?"

"Positively final. There is nothing more to be said. I have heard you through, and my decision will not be changed. Now, gentlemen, good-night."

"One moment."

Assistant Secretary Randolph Morten's quiet words turned Z-7 and Operator 5. He had not moved from his position near the door. He had not for a second taken his eyes from Jimmy Christopher. Now his gaze was coolly confident, challenging. A faint, contemptuous smile curved his lips.

"Perhaps there is a detail which Operator 5 may be permitted to handle, Mr. Secretary. Here is a dispatch which has come in over our teletypes since they left WDC-13. Since this office is now intercepting all Intelligence reports, they do not yet know of it. It concerns an espionage agent at work in this country."

"Yes, Morten?" the Secretary asked impatiently, while Operator 5 studied the Assistant's crafty eyes. "What is it?"

"It mentions," Morten answered slowly, "a woman spy known as Mayla Lazare."

JIMMY CHRISTOPHER'S nerves tightened as Morten handed a dispatch to him. The notations on it indicated it had been sent by secret cable from a sub-headquarters of the Intelligence in Europe. It stated briefly:

> WDC-13... INFORMATION JUST VERIFIED THAT SPY MAYLA LAZARE IS WORKING IN WASHINGTON UNDER NAME OF ROSITA ALBAN... ONCE CLOSE FRIEND OF BASIL VON PRAAG... RECOMMEND CAREFUL INVESTIGATION... CB.

"Mayla Lazare, I believe," Morten continued suavely, "is a Balkarian, and we need not worry about a clash with the Balkarian government. The suggested investigation might unearth an interesting connection. I already have taken from our records the address of the woman known as Señorita Rosita Alban. I suggest that Operator 5 try to discover why she is at work in Washington now."

Jimmy Christopher's gaze sharpened. The daring of Randolph Morten startled him anew. Only a few short hours ago the Assistant Secretary had sipped coffee at the side of the notorious Mayla Lazare; now he was pretending to know nothing of her. Morten's suggestion that Operator 5 investigate the woman spy was one approach toward the hidden espionage ring with which Morten himself was unquestionably associated; yet the Assistant Secretary dared open it. For use as a trap!

"Perhaps," the Assistant Secretary asked quietly, "you do not care to undertake this detail, young man?"

Grimly, Jimmy Christopher answered: "I will gladly accept it—with the permission of the Secretary."

"On Morten's recommendation," the Secretary answered impatiently, "you may have my permission for that."

Z-7 strode to the door as Jimmy Christopher continued to study the enigmatic smile on Morten's face. More keenly with every second he became certain that the Assistant Secretary was planning his destruction. He paused on the sill as Morten's voice came again—a purr.

"You will report to me, young man?"

"Whatever results from this investigation, Mr. Morten,"

Jimmy Christopher answered cryptically, "you will promptly learn."

"I," Morten retorted with lips twinkling contemptuously, "wish you the greatest of luck."

THE UNITED STATES was opening its eyes to the startling and appalling facts that among all the great powers of the world, she was most weakly defended.

Complacently, the more than one hundred million souls of the nation had thought nothing of this vital matter; but now, day by day, they were seeing, to their dismay, their country's armed helplessness.

"Should the United States face an active war today," declared Brigadier-General Hartwell, Assistant Chief of Staff, War Plans Division, over a coast-to-coast radio hook-up while feverish interest in the subject swept the country, "should she be called upon to defend herself from an aggressor, she would beyond all doubt find herself a victim of her own carelessness.

"Not only would our machines of war face an enemy far better equipped, far more powerful, but we would find ourselves cut off from foreign sources of war materials—defeated by our own shortsightedness! Almost any great nation, by the simple act of forbidding the shipment of war materials to the United States in a crisis, can cripple us—pronounce upon us a sentence of doom!"

The Chief of Staff of the Joint Board of the U.S. Army and Navy, in an exclusive interview granted to Diane Elliot through the Amalgamated Press, issued a warning to the people that their will and theirs alone must decide the fate of the nation.

"The Armament Bills being prepared for Congressional

action are the most vital in the history of the United States," he declared in part. "Upon them rests entirely the far-flung program proposed for the strengthening of our Army and Navy and Air Corps. The inevitable struggle over these measures in our Congressional Halls is certain to be bitter, and it will be won only by a narrow margin. It is not the personal opinions of the representatives, but the will of the people they represent, which must decide the issue. The momentous problem is squarely up to every man and woman in the country.

"Shall we or shall we not allow the United States to continue to be the weakling of the world among the great powers? Shall we remain in constant danger of certain defeat, in case of aggression, or shall we strengthen ourselves so that we may fearlessly face any foe? Shall we preserve our nation, or doom it to extinction? That is the great question which we must decide once and for all, and now!"

Feverish interest in the impending legislation heightened from coast to coast as more and more of the startling facts were revealed. Bitter contests began in newspapers, and over nationwide broadcasting hook-ups. The problem affecting the lives and homes and families and futures of every man, woman and child became uppermost in the mind of the nation. Even more amazing than the revelations of the weakness of the U.S. defenses came the information that, even while our strength waned,

Americans were aiding in increasing the belligerent power of foreign nations!*

Across the country flooded printed appeals arguing both sides of the momentous problem. Long-standing friends found themselves bitterly at odds on the question. Those who opposed

---

* AUTHOR's NOTE: In contrast to the sad condition of the United States Air Corps, it is true that Russia has not only the largest army in the world, but her air force is the greatest air fleet in the world today. What is even more startling is that the United States has aided Russia materially in the building up of her gigantic war air fleet.

That Russia is mobilizing this powerful air force with the aid of military secrets that came from American munitions firms, Senate investigators learned as long ago as last September. The special arms investigating committee obtained information that millions of dollars were spent in perfecting the inventions which the Soviet Republic is utilizing through purchases from United States airplane building companies. Investigators revealed that a number of American aviation engineers are in Russia helping to establish this greatest air force in the world.

At the same time the Senate munitions investigating committee revealed that smuggled American machine guns, revolvers and ammunition are used by Adolph Hitler's Nazis and other political groups in strife-torn Germany. Thompson machine-guns and small arms have been smuggled into German in large quantities, along with munitions from other countries, through Holland and other nearby nations, according to letters put into the record. These revelations mean that while the United States defenses remain woefully inadequate, munitions manufactured in the United States are being used to strengthen the militaristic power of foreign nations!

the measure rushed into print, to the microphones of the great broadcasting chains, to plead peace through disarmament. Hour by hour the conflicting factions marshaled their strength. Millions of words, pro and con, began to stream from roaring presses and from powerful radio antennae—while, unknown to the millions who read and listened, hidden beneath the surface of everyday life, relentless secret forces came to grips.

IN THE streets of Washington, on a night not long after the gala Embassy Ball, newsboys ran shouting late editions.

"General Hartwell pleads for armed strength on death-bed! Suddenly taken ill but still fights for bigger defenses!"

"Coast to coast hookup fails during rearmament talk! Sabotage suspected!"

"Admiral Thornton, champion of stronger defense, mysteriously missing!"

The cries of the running boys did not penetrate into a small room located near the great, domed Capitol of the nation. Darkness lay along the streets outside; thicker darkness filled it. It remained soundless—until the faint noise of an opening door disturbed the quiet.

A man entered the dark room hesitantly. He paused just beyond the sill, and was startled by a sharp click which announced immediately that the door was shut. Promptly he tried the knob, found it locked. He sensed that an electrical device, operated from a point beyond, had drawn a catch into the socket. He stood uneasily in the gloom, waiting during an uncertain moment.

A mysterious summons had brought him to this room—an

unsigned message which urged complete secrecy upon him. He had followed strange directions to reach this door which had now fastened behind him—directions which offered no explanation. An uncanny urge had led him to follow them: and now, in the dark room, not knowing why he was present, he waited.

A faint glow appeared a few yards away—a point of light which glimmered into brightness. The glare of an electric bulb turned upon him. A shade, cupping it, left the wielder obscured in shadow.

The man whom it was exposing, strove to peer beyond it. His head was bandaged, his face gaunt, his lips curved bitterly. He was one who had been, but was no longer, K-2 of the United States Intelligence.

Now, in the shadow behind the light, K-2 glimpsed a ghostly outline. A man was standing there in the gloom—or was it a man? A man, or some strange thing that—? Drawn irresistibly, K-2 stepped closer. When he paused, near the light, he was peering at an apparition startling to look upon.

Though it was garbed in a plain black suit, its head was a fleshless skull! Its hands, protruding from the black sleeves, seemed to be dry bones! A clothed skeleton—and yet it had eyes! Its eyes glittered deep in shadowed sockets, studying the amazed K-2.

The ex-operator of the Intelligence knew that the light was tricking him—knew that the head of this unknown man was covered by a cloth mask painted to the semblance of a skull, that the hands were merely covered with black gloves painted so that the fingers seemed to be bare bones—yet the uncanny effect filled him with cold fascination.

Breathily he asked: "Who are you? Why have you called me here?"

The living skeleton said softly: "Who I am must remain unknown to you. I am your friend. I trust you as I wish you to trust me. I have called you here so that you may have the honor of becoming the first of a secret organization—an undercover organization to be known as the Hidden Hundred."

K-2 stood speechless in wonderment. From the living skull the soft voice continued—and to each word K-2 listened with growing wonder. Out of his uncertainty came eagerness. Out of his doubt came conviction. At last the voice ceased, and one skeleton hand reached forward into the light. The bony fingers opened....

"Look!"

K-2 peered into the white palm, at a glittering object lying there. His widened eyes rose again to those glimmering in the sockets of the white death's-head. Again the hushed voice spoke.

"Now—do you understand? For your allegiance to the Hidden Hundred you will receive no payment save the satisfaction that you are serving your deepest loyalty. You may be ordered to break law after law. You will certainly find yourself a pariah, a man who must live a living death in deepest secrecy. You will be hunted, in constant danger. These things you must realize before you answer my one question to you.

"Do you pledge your undying loyalty, once and forever, to the Hidden Hundred?"

K-2's eyes blazed as he blurted: "Once and forever, I swear my allegiance to the Hidden Hundred!"

Out of the shadow the skeleton hand again reached. K-2 gripped it—not a thing of cold, dry hone, but firm, warm flesh. The gloved fingers trembled with a desperate sincerity... then the hand withdrew. The light dimmed. Again the amazed K-2 found himself standing in deepest darkness—and he sensed that the presence was gone.

CHAPTER 7
TRAITOR'S TRAP

OPERATOR 5 strode briskly from the secret elevator entrance to the level of WDC-13, through the inner door, and straight to the desk of Z-7. The Washington chief's stubby fingers were drumming his desk while he read reports. He came to his feet tensely as Jimmy Christopher entered.

"Damnable!" he exploded. "Here's a report that General Hartwell has just died—poisoning again suspected—a violent thirst the only symptom. Another saying that Admiral Frankson—Chief of the Bureau of Aeronautics, Navy—has committed suicide. A shot through the head—dead. Dead by his own hand—that man? I don't believe it!"

"Nor I, Chief," Jimmy Christopher agreed. "Frankson's death costs us the most ardent advocate of a stronger air force in the country today. He knew, better than any other man perhaps, the deplorable condition of our flying defenses." *

"And we can do nothing about it—nothing!" Z-7 snapped. "Every time I make an approach toward the espionage ring, the Secretary of State orders me off. I cannot criticize his motives— he is absolutely sincere, entirely above suspicion, an admirable man—but his methods are paralyzing us. I have just completed the job of dismissing every man whose name he checked on our roster—and I feel that I've committed exactly so many different murders.

"What the devil can our discharged men do?" he went on heatedly. "Most of them have spent long years in the Service. They came in young. They're finding themselves now with-

---

* Author's Note: Our Army Air Corps so wretchedly and tragically failed to meet the Air Mail emergency and subsequent investigation revealed that, in its present miserable condition, the Air Corps was utterly ineffective as a means of defense.

Under our present national policy toward military aviation, our swiftest and best army fighters rank sixth among the fighting planes of the world and are unable even to reach similar foreign aircraft to engage them in battle!

If we were to put all our Navy planes in the air at once, 25 per cent of the pilots in the air would be flying training planes. It is estimated that if we were to gather together all the planes of the Navy and the Army, we would actually have no more than 600 planes of any decent service quality according to 1935 standards.

These startling facts are totally unknown to the average American though his security depends vitally upon the defenses affected.

out business experience, without any training except a highly specialized one which is useless to them in ordinary life. Those men won't be able to find decent jobs. They'll go hungry. They'll break. God, I hate to think of what will happen to those men!"

"I think I know, Chief," Operator 5 said quietly, "what is happening to them."

Z-7 seemed not to hear; his bitterness absorbed him. He looked up to ask: "What are you doing with the detail Morten gave you, Operator 5?"

"I've been watching the house in which Mayla Lazare lives. Just now Tim's relieving me. I'm feeling my way very cautiously on those orders. Morten's trying to trap me, Chief."

"I know!"

"His purpose, at the very least, is to involve me so the Secretary of State will be obliged to eject me from the Service for disobedience. He deliberately placed me in a dilemma. So far I've been watching sharp—but the moment's coming when I shall act. Chief, I said, a moment ago, that I think I know what our ex-Intelligence men are doing."

"What do you mean?"

"I've reason to believe they're forming a secret organization among themselves. They are, I think, being drawn together, under cover, by an unknown leader. What their purpose is, I cannot report, but I know something very strange is in the wind."

Z-7's black eyes smoldered. "Organizing? My old men organizing? How do you know?"

"I've seen some of our ex-operators acting strangely. I've noticed a number of agents in Washington who were posted in the south and west. For some reason, all those discharged are gathering in Washington. Something extraordinary is behind it, Chief—depend on that!"

Z-7 JERKED to his feet in alarm. From a file cabinet he brought quickly a folder of reports, scanned them, then peered piercingly at Operator 5.

"Is it possible," he asked huskily, "that they are connected in some way with—" He broke off, carefully considering. "Operator 5, you're familiar with these reports. Five different Embassies have been entered at night, their safes opened and secret documents stolen. Homes have been robbed. Consuls have been held up and searched and some of their papers taken. This is all the work of some organization identified with a strange mark sometimes left at the scene of the crime. A Roman numeral eleven."

Z-7 stroked it quickly on a scratchpad: XI.

"By God!" His eyes blazed. "That symbol may not mean eleven at all. The X may stand for the prefix ex-. The I may be the initial of Intelligence. You're right, Operator 5! My old operators have organized themselves into a band of espionage agents operating independently—without credentials!"

"That, Chief, is a serious matter."

"Serious?" Z-7 snapped. "They're guilty of criminal acts. They can be considered only as enemies of the country, no matter what their purposes may be. You've hit upon a vital matter. If those men are undertaking to handle cases forbidden to us, our orders from the Secretary necessitate that we stamp them out. I intend to consult with him at once concerning this. In the meantime—"

"Yes, Chief?" Operator 5 spoke quietly. "Orders?"

"Orders!" Z-7 barked. "Follow your lead. Learn the place where those men are meeting. Find out, above everything else, who their leader is. Report to me immediately when you obtain that information!"

Z-7 snatched up the telephone and snapped into the transmitter: "Get me the Secretary of State at once!"

Jimmy Christopher nodded a quiet "Yes sir" and turned on his heel. As he left the office and went toward the secret elevator, he heard the rasping tones of the chief speaking over the wire. Z-7 was telling the Secretary of State the first facts to reach the Intelligence concerning the undercover organization which called itself the Hidden Hundred.

Even at that moment, at a remote point in the nation's Capital, the Hidden Hundred were met in secret conclave....

NO SOUND entered the dark room. Not a spark of light broke the blackness that filled it. In the gloom a man stood waiting, alone.

Alone—and yet he sensed presence in the dark. He felt, uncannily, that eyes were upon him. He faced the uncertainty without a tremor, for long years of service in the U.S. Intelligence had removed any capacity for fear. He was one who had been designated R-9 in the service, but his name was no longer written upon the secret roster of WDC-13.

Like K-2, he had been summoned to this strange rendezvous by an unsigned, mysterious message. Like K-2, he had felt drawn to keep it. Like K-2 he now saw a glimmer of light before him, which brightened steadily, which shielded an uncertain figure. When his sight cleared he saw vaguely the figure which K-2 had seen first among all those who had become members of the Hidden Hundred—a living being with the skull and the claws of a skeleton!

A soft voice spoke, and R-9 listened. In amazement he heard revelations which would have appalled him while he had served in the Intelligence; but now he listened with grim satisfaction. For long moments the hushed voice spoke until at last a bony hand reached into the light, cupped and holding a tiny object. R-9 peered at it; his startled gaze flashed upward to the eyes shining from the sockets in the head of the living skull.

"I have told you of the dangers you face," the voice resumed in a whisper. "I have made plain to you that your orders will make you a hunted criminal. I must add now that already the Intelligence has learned of our organization through your former comrade Operator 5, and that Z-7 is taking steps to crush the Hidden Hundred under the command of the Secretary of State. Your pledge to us will make you not only a spy, but even worse, a spy without a country.

"Realizing this, can you swear your undying allegiance, once and forever, to the Hidden Hundred?"

"I do! I promise everlasting faith to the Hidden Hundred!"

Somehow the eyes in the sockets of the skull seemed grimly to smile. "To you," the hushed voice came "falls the honor of completing our organization. No one else will be added to our ranks except to fill the vacancies of members who are snatched from us by capture or death. Once you were known as R-9. Now you are designated X-100."

Again the skeleton hand of the leader of the Hidden Hundred

reached into the light. The man who had that moment become X-100 gripped it fervently—a hand, not of bone, but of hard flesh. It withdrew slowly; and suddenly a swishing sound filled the room.

X-100 turned quickly to see a black curtain drawing aside. Beyond, in the opened space, he perceived a company of phantoms—row upon row of silent men, all wearing the skull mask, all peering with eyes deep-set in bony sockets, all extending their claws for the clasp that would seal, once and forever, X-100's pledge.

One by one they came forward. One after another silently seized the hand of X-100 and withdrew. The last—one designated X-99—brought to the recruit a mask fashioned of black cloth, and a pair of gloves. Quickly X-100 pulled them on. His hands, like those of the ninety-nine, became bare bones. His head, like others, became a skull. Indistinguishable from those others now, he peered at the corner where the leader of the Hidden Hundred had heard his vow of allegiance. The blackness was empty there....

IN THE gloom of the outlying street Operator 5 stood concealed. Backed into a doorway, he watched the sordid tenement across the way. Its windows were lightless; it looked deserted; but he knew it was not. Stationed here, he had seen men slip into that dwelling one after another—men he knew to be ex-Intelligence agents, assembling in secret meeting. Now, during a long period of emptiness, he waited without a moment's relaxation in his vigilance.

He tightened when the front entrance of the tenement

opened. Two men hurried from it, glanced around furtively, and walked quickly away. Another pair appeared; another and another. Operator 5 glimpsed their faces as they emerged score after score, in pairs. None of them glimpsed him or suspected that he was watching; they scattered in the darkness. It was not until Jimmy Christopher's count was near one hundred that he tensed for action.

While two men walked quickly along the street, he followed, without sound, on the opposite side. One of them was an ex-Intelligence agent known as S-8; that man Operator 5 had selected to trail. Expertly keeping himself out of sight, he followed until S-8 slipped into a light sedan, signaling good night to his companion. Jimmy Christopher waited until the car started up, then swung swiftly around the corner and sprang to the wheel of his Diesel-engined roadster.

Twisting back, he followed the car in which S-8 was encircling one of the avenues. The trail passed across Washington, presently led into a neighborhood remote and dark. At last S-8 drew the sedan to the curb, alighted and looked around quickly. He gave Operator 5's roadster only a glance, for it had drawn swiftly to the curb and its lights had winked out. In it Jimmy Christopher watched S-8 mount the steps of an old house.

Surprise chilled him as he noted the number above the door—1740. Surprise, because the orders given him by Randolph Morten included a number on this street—1742. And 1742, in which lived the notorious woman spy called Mayla Lazare, was directly next door to the house which had just been entered by a man who was both an ex-Intelligence operator and a member of the Hidden Hundred!

Jimmy Christopher slipped from the wheel. Quickly he moved along the opposite sidewalk. Suddenly he turned, bounded up steps, thrust open a door. He entered a house musty with emptiness. Secretly he had used it as an observation post during his watch of 1742. As he turned toward the door of the front room it opened quickly and Tim Donovan appeared.

"Gee, I'm glad you're back, Jimmy! I've missed you. There's nothing to report about 1742."

Operator 5 answered quietly as he stepped into the room. "But our watchful waiting must end tonight. I've got to take the chance of walking into the trap Morten has set for me."

An electric lantern was burning in the empty room; it threw his huge shadow on the wall as he peeled up a tiny flap cut in the window-blind and peered through. For a long moment he studied the two houses opposite: and when he turned away, his eyes were dark with thought.

"It's a dangerous battle, Tim. The Rearmament Bills are growing into a greater issue with every passing hour. It's impossible to say now which side will win the contest. It's possible—very possible—that the people will rise against the bills and doom the country to defenselessness—not knowing that they've been influenced by a diabolical espionage ring."

"But why, Jimmy?" Tim Donovan asked quickly. "How can anyone think it's better to be weak than strong?"

Operator 5's lips tightened. "Many of our greatest leaders believe the vast expenditures are unnecessary," he answered.

"The rearmament measures will cost gigantic sums if they're enacted. It will mean heavier taxes—and already taxes are a burden on the people.* Make no mistake about it, Tim—there

---

* AUTHOR's NOTE: The opponents of military preparedness for the United States possess a strong argument in the unanswerable contention that the new military program will result in increasing taxation which is already a heavy burden upon the American people.

The proportion of taxes levied by national, state and local governments to the total income of the United States has been increasing continuously since 1925 until today it amounts to 20.7 per cent, according to figures just issued by the National Industrial Conference Board.

"Directly or indirectly," according to Percy H. Johnston, president of the Chemical Bank and Trust Company, "the average American working a full five-day week, works all Monday and part of Tuesday morning to pay his taxes."

At the tax conference of the American Management Association it was brought out that one corporation, doing business in thirty-five states pays 198 separate taxes. So great an expense has the circulation and paying of these taxes become, with clerical and legal work involved, that a business representative on the floor of Congress alleged that the American taxpayers are paying $400,000,000 a year over and above the amount of taxes for the work of paying them!

The American people are now paying nine and one-half thousand millions of dollars a year in taxes. This is one-fifth of the national income. Governmental expenditures already approximate annually fifteen and one-half thousand million dollars. In the last five years the gross public debt of the

are powerful arguments on both sides—and it's impossible to foresee the outcome."

AGAIN HE peered through the peephole. Afterward he paced nervously back and forth, the Irish lad's eyes following him anxiously. Presently he paused, and the eager expression on the boy's face caused him to smile. Quietly he said:

"I know what you're waiting for, Tim—a new trick. Perhaps I'll have time to show you one."

"Gee, Jimmy, you can't show too many to suit me! Maybe you won't be able to fool me this time!"

"We'll see about that, old-timer."

Operator 5 smiled as he drew, from his coat pocket, three colored ribbons. He gave them over one after another for examination, and Tim found them to be quite ordinary. Each was a different color—red, blue, yellow. He drew out a handkerchief and tossed that to the boy also.

"A little experiment," he explained, "to show how sensitive the sense of touch may become if properly developed. I'll endeavor to detect the different colors of the ribbons by feeling alone. First, Tim, blindfold me tightly."

United States has increased about fourteen thousand million dollars. Our public debt will soon total thirty-four thousand million dollars.

Furthermore, the American business man knows the failure of Disarmament Conference means that between three hundred million and four hundred million dollars a year will be added to the tax burden of the country.

The weighty arguments on both sides of this vital question testify to its vast importance.

Eagerly the boy did so.

"Now merely hand me any one of the ribbons you choose. In order to convince you that I don't peek, I'll turn my back when you give it to me, and keep it behind me all the time. Through my fingertips I'll be able to see the color of the ribbon you chose. Okay—let's go!"

Operator 5 turned his back on the boy; and again Tim keenly inspected the three colored ribbons. They were all of the same silk and, feeling them, he could detect no difference whatever. Convinced that there was nothing suspicious about them, he selected one, thrust the others into his pocket, and placed it in the hands of Operator 5.

Jimmy Christopher turned to face Tim and kept the chosen ribbon behind his back. "I simply feel the ribbon," he said quietly, "and tell the color. Red, you see, is a hard color. Blue is soft, and yellow has a quality of its own. You have given me, Tim, the blue ribbon!"

"That's right, Jimmy!" the boy blurted. "Gee, how'd you do it? Let me try it again!"

Operator 5 agreed promptly.

The trick was repeated five times. Each time he promptly and correctly named the color of the chosen ribbon. When he removed the handkerchief he found the boy puzzling over the three strips, completely baffled.

"You've got me guessing," he sighed.

Operator 5 stepped again to the hidden flap in the window blind, peered through. Minutely he studied the front of the two mysterious houses across the way. Then he turned back, to see Tim still fingering the ribbons. He smiled.

"It's very simple, Tim. They are of exactly the same material, of the same width—but of slightly different lengths. That's the whole secret!"

In amazement Tim compared the lengths of the three strands and found it to be true. But, still bewildered, he asked: "How can you tell from that, Jimmy?"

"Easy, Tim!" Operator 5 chuckled. "When I hold the selected ribbon behind my back, I place one end between my thumb and the base of my forefinger and hold it like that. Then I simply wind the ribbon around my hand. That's a means of measuring it. The end of the red ribbon, you see, when I've finished winding, comes to my thumb." He demonstrated as he spoke. "Winding the blue the same way, the end of it comes halfway across my hand. In the case of the yellow, again winding it the same way, the end comes to the little finger. That's absolutely all there is to it, Tim—but it's very baffling, isn't it?"

"I'll say it is! You had me fooled!"

Operator 5 chuckled. "When you perform the trick, always handle the ribbons rolled. That is, don't let them dangle so your audience can see they're of different lengths. Take them up coiled, and hand them back coiled, and have them examined one by one so they can't be compared. There's a whole series of tricks of the same sort—detecting different colors apparent by touch. There's one with paper tags, another with matches, another with marbles."

"Show 'em to me now, Jimmy!"

"Later, Tim." Operator 5 spoke quietly. "I promise you I'll show them all to you soon,* but tonight I've got an important job to do. Mr. Randolph Morten has set a trap for me—and I can't wait any longer. I'm going to walk into it deliberately."

HIS VOICE faded as he opened the door; and Tim Donovan stared after him in dismay. He vanished in the darkness of the entrance even as the boy called anxiously. He did not pause. He stepped into the gloom of the street and walked briskly. He felt the eye of Tim Donovan upon him—knew that the worried boy was peering through the peep-hole in the blind. He strode to the corner, crossed, and rapidly approached the two sinister houses.

A plan of action had formed in his mind, and now he unhesitantly followed it. Striding past 1742, the home of the notorious Mayla Lazare; he turned abruptly to the entrance of 1740, into which the ex-Intelligence agent had gone. Melting into the darkness of the entrance, he listened. No sound. From his pocket he removed a pack of keys—master implements made in his workshop, capable of opening any known type of lock. Deftly he tried three—and the third opened the way. He stepped alertly, nerves stretched tight, into an utterly black hall.

A deep, intense silence filled the house. Operator 5 moved quietly through the darkness. He found stairs and mounted them, intently listening. Then he ascended to a third floor. At every step he felt that the dwelling was empty but that a moment

---

* AUTHOR's NOTE: Operator 5's promise to perform and explain these color-divination feats of magic will be kept in forthcoming adventures.

ago it had been occupied. When he turned to descend he deliberately snapped switches to light the way.

Lamps disclosed garish furnishings. A quick inspection of the rooms opening off the hallways convinced him that the ex-Intelligence agent was no longer in the house. He was certain his man had not left by the front entrance. A moment's inspection of the knob of the rear door showed dust on it, and he knew it had not been touched. Eyes sharp, he again went up and down the stairs, inspecting the wall which separated 1742 from 1740.

His search led him to a doorway beneath the first-floor flight. He opened it upon darkness, and damp air gusted around him. Slipping his fountain-pen torch from his pocket, he peered down a flight of steps that were dusty—and saw the dust marked by new footprints. Silence held below. Soundlessly, his torch playing a thin beam through the gloom, Jimmy Christopher descended.

At the base of the flight he stood motionless, his light probing into the corners. Packing-cases were piled on every side, along every wall. Again he drew close to the wall, which evidently separated this basement from that of the house next door. His light disclosed no partition, no crack that might betray a secret passage. But, against the bricks, more packing-cases were piled and as he tapped them a hollow reverberation told him that while all the others were filled these were empty.

He attempted to draw them away; but they would not move. His fingers strayed over the bricks, the boards, searching. Suddenly his nerves tensed—a low, grinding sound disturbed the quiet. Alertly he stepped back, watching the pile of crates swing forward. A panel of bricks, to which they were bolted, moved with them, disclosing an opening in the wall and a bright light burning beyond.

He listened tensely while the hidden door swung wide. Quickly, as the panel began to pivot shut again, he dragged a small case forward. The square of bricks struck it and stopped; the way remained open. His hand stealing to his arm-pitted automatic, his eyes glittering dark, Jimmy Christopher stepped through.

AT ONCE he stopped short, peering at the farther half of the cellar of 1740. A partition, built of iron pipes cemented into the walls and the floor, and covered with heavy screen, divided the basement into two sections. There was no door in the wall of screen, no opening of any kind; but below it, in the enclosure, there was a flutter of movement.

A rustling, hissing sound chilled Jimmy Christopher's blood. He stepped forward to see glistening things coiling over the straw-matted floor toward the partition. Snakes! Their evil bodies gleamed in the bright light as they writhed near the screen; and their heads raised. Fangs glittered in the light, and the ominous markings of spread hoods shone. The hissing was the vicious defiance of king cobras!

He retreated grimly, as the malevolent eyes of the reptiles gleamed his way. He examined to make sure there was no door nor window opening into the den. Among the tufting straw he saw black coils, slithering darkness. He counted twenty of the poisonous things and knew more must be hidden in the straw. With a shudder he retreated, peering around.

A stairway led up one wall of the cellar; and around it other packing-cases were piled. One of them had been broken open and almost emptied. He saw that it had been full of printed pamphlets. Quickly he inspected it. The document was a plea for disarmament, an impassioned argument against the impending Arms Bills. And it bore the name, as author, of the Rev. J. Gregory Whitehouse.

Operator 5's eyes darkened ominously. The Rev. Whitehouse was world-famous, a crusading Man of God, whose radio broadcasts aligned millions of devotees behind him on vital issues. If Whitehouse had written this plea, Operator 5 knew, he had sold out to the espionage ring! If he had not, it was a diabolical forgery. Jimmy Christopher saw indications that the pamphlet had not been printed in the United States, and sensed anew the vast extent of the under-cover work of the power that was fighting to keep his own nation defenseless.

That millions of copies of this subversive document had been circulated secretly about the country he had no doubt. That it was marshaling millions against the Arms Bills he was certain. He went cold with the realization.

Grimly he turned to the stairs leading upward. Step by step he mounted, soundlessly. At the door he paused, hearing voices so faint he could not distinguish word from word. The knob turned in his hand; he peered into a gloomy hallway. Now he located the voices in a room at the rear. Quickly he crossed the carpeted hall, toward the door of the adjoining room. He looked into darkness, glided over the sill, and directed cautious steps toward the rear wall.

The voices became distinct. One, rumbling, he recognized as that of Peter Keeve. Keeve's startling statement was clearly audible now—and Jimmy Christopher's blood went cold when he heard it. "They're meeting now—full twenty important leaders of the rearmament movement, in the offices of the General Staff. They're planning their great campaign tonight. They do not know that at midnight they all—every man of them—will die!"

QUICKLY JIMMY CHRISTOPHER glanced at his watch. The time was precisely eleven-sixteen. "At midnight they all will die!" Keeve had asserted; and midnight was but forty-four minutes away.

Bewildered, appalled, Operator 5 listened as a second voice spoke. He recognized it as that of the ex-Intelligence operative once designated D-4, who had entered the adjoining house and stolen into this one through the hidden door.

"Kill twenty men in one blow? How is it possible! God! You can't—!"

"My friend," Keeve answered, "you do not comprehend the power of our organization. Let it suffice that one of our best agents, Lebow, found his way into the office of the General Staff less than twenty-four hours ago, in the dead of night. He carried with him a very interesting device—and left it there. It's concealed in a locked file cabinet. Its clockwork mechanism is adjusted so that, at precisely midnight tonight, while the twenty armament leaders are meeting, an electrical spark will set off a powerful charge of explosive. No man in that room can possibly survive!

"But this, my friend, is not your concern. It's your purpose to learn the identities of the men who make up the Hidden Hundred. Especially are you to find out who the leader of that organization is. We'll make short work of him—and it, I promise you!"

"I haven't seen the face of the leader!" the man who was once D-4 declared desperately. "I can't be sure that—"

"You will make sure, my friend," the voice of Keeve said ominously, "or you will be the first of the Hidden Hundred to die!"

A silence followed—a pause which was broken by a woman's voice. Mayla Lazare declared: "You need fear us only if you fail. If you serve us well, you will be safe—and rich. You know now that the power of Randolph Morten is great—and it protects us."

Again Keeve: "It is now only forty minutes until the twenty leaders of the Arms Bills will—shall I say—abandon their cause?"

The sound of an opening door startled Operator 5. He whirled, and strode toward the entrance of the dark room. His blood froze as, near at hand, he heard a swishing of skirts. Mayla Lazare was walking directly toward the door behind which he stood. Following her came the heavy tramp of Keeve.

Jimmy Christopher's mind raced. Then, choosing to slip out without having been seen—if possible—he darted deeper into the darkness.

His hand snatched open a closet door as the shadowed figure of the woman appeared in the dim light of the hall. He retreated, closing it. Breathless, he stood back in the confined space while

126

the light, slow footfalls of the woman came toward him. His heart stopped suddenly when he heard metal rasp. A key turned in the lock of the closet!

Through the panels the voice of Mayla Lazare came with ominous softness. "We have long been expecting you, Operator 5!"

And suddenly Jimmy Christopher felt the floor yielding beneath his feet. Gradually one edge was lowering, sloping downward at an increasing angle.

He backed, startled, as light glared up in his eyes from a cavity below. He glimpsed a bed of straw—wriggling black reptiles. The cage of cobras lay directly below. And all support was swinging away—the entire floor of the closet was lowering like a trapdoor.

A light, taunting laugh reached his ears through the panels, as he groped frantically for the hooks screwed to the wall of the closet. He gripped one on each side and pulled himself up— while the floor lowered completely away. He hung breathless, peering down into that reptilian hell.

"We've known since the moment you entered the house, Operator 5," a new voice came through the panels—that of Peter Keeve. "It's pleased us to let you learn of our plans for tonight. Our friend Morten planned carefully to trap you here—did he not?" Keeve's laugh boomed.

Operator 5's muscles burned as he supported himself on the hooks. Desperately he attempted, with his feet, to find a crevice however small that would be an aid to support. There was no wainscoting at the base of the closet walls—nothing but smooth

Down into the light toward that hideous waiting death Operator 5 dropped!

plaster. Not the slightest means of keeping out of the cage of reptiles except the hooks to which he had fastened his hands. The sharp metal bit into his palms and fingers—and as he felt them yielding, he peered up in dismay.

Down into the light toward that hideous waiting death Operator 5 dropped!

The screws of the hooks were pulling slowly out of the plaster!

"You promised to report to Assistant Secretary Morten?" the acrid voice of Mayla Lazare came again. "You accepted his challenge? Now, I think, you must regret it!"

A groan of desperation broke from his lips. Suddenly the hook to which his right hand was clamped pulled out! He lurched against the opposite wall, dangling by one arm—and as suddenly the second hook broke free. He was falling.

CHAPTER 8
TICKING DOOM

I N THAT swift, desperate moment, his moves were like lightning. He had lost his automatic when the floor had slipped from beneath him, now it lay among the cobras. His right hand streaked to the only other weapon he carried: his rapier. He clicked the belt buckle loose, whipped the flexible scabbard away.

The steel flashed in the light as his feet struck the bed of straw. He swirled the blade swiftly about and the razor edge slashed to a darting black head. Blood colored the blade—a snake head flew off. At the same instant his springy muscles flung him backward toward the heavy screen wall.

Each step was a threat of death from a reptile possibly concealed in the tufting straw. His rapier whipped back and forth and the stuff flew in a storm as he cleared the way. Back to the screen, he turned to see the black death crawling toward him. His swift movements had aroused hissing defiance from every corner of the cage. Straw rustled with glistening black movements; glassy eyes gleamed; within the cage drew a closing circle of doom. He stepped forward alertly; and again his *épée* whipped out. The body of another snake writhed in pieces, coloring the straw with its blood.

A swift glance upward showed him faces in the light, malevolent eyes staring down. The door of the closet had been opened; Peter Keeve and Mayla Lazare were peering in cold fury. The man's voice roared:

"He'll kill them all! I'll make shorter work of him—with bullets!"

A gun blasted in the floorless closet; a bullet whined past his head. He sprang back, out of range of Keeve, lashing his rapier again. His swift strokes protected him from the advancing, crawling death. Coldly desperate, he whirled against the screen while the noise of an opening door rattled through the basement—a sound which signaled Keeve's approach from a new direction.

One sharp thrust drove the slender blade of the rapier through the screen. Sawing against the tough strands, he bore downward, making a slit as Keeve bounded upon the stairs. Hissing death threatened from behind; blasting doom threatened from the steps. He slashed with his rapier again, tore the flaps aside, wrenched through at the moment Keeve whirled to fire.

A rocking report reverberated through the basement; flame flashed. Operator 5 sprang forward, whipping his blade overhead. The singing steel struck the bulb of the single electric globe. Instantly fragments of glass rained across the basement and the place was dark. The flash of another shot cut the gloom as he whirled toward Keeve—and at that moment, outlined by the light through the door, the traitorous ex-agent D-4 bounded down, automatic in hand.

Jimmy Christopher's *épée* slashed desperately toward Keeve. There was a scream of dismay; the keen edge had found the spy's gun-hand. A desperate shot followed; a bullet spat past Operator 5's face, and the glare limned the ferocious face of Keeve. The spy, arm cut to the bone, was backing up. D-4 sped down the stairs as Jimmy Christopher sprang aside, whipping Keeve away with another desperate flick of the blade.

A NOTHER SHOT! Into its rattling echoes came a scream from the bearded lips of Keeve. Operator 5's rapier darted to the spot at which the flame had flashed. Steel sparkled against steel during a swift moment that ended with a gasp from the man who had been D-4. The ex-agent's automatic thumped from his paralyzed hand; and in the gloom Jimmy Christopher stood with glittering blade poised to thrust.

"A traitor to the United States!" Operator 5 denounced him acidly. "A traitor even to the Hidden Hundred!"

The ex-agent staggered, face ashen in the dim light. Suddenly he whirled, to run in terror.

Operator 5 leaped back into the darkness. A prolonged moan sounded in the gloom as he bounded to the still open secret door in the connecting wall. Another shrill scream followed. He paused, blade uplifted, and put his fountain-pen torch again into use.

Its thin beam shot through the darkness and disclosed Keeve lying panting on the floor. Near him two hooded cobras weaved erect, fangs glinting, glassy eyes shining with triumph. They had crawled out through the slits in the screen, had struck in the dark at Keeve. Now, rolling in torture, he strove to escape the glistening black things and instantly one of them struck again, leaving two livid spots above the black beard on his cheek!

Operator 5 leaped back as D-4 rushed crazily for the open door. His light swung again, to disclose D-4 spilling to the floor. A cobra's fangs were fastened on the ex-agent's ankle. In his desperate flight he had carried the reptile with him as it clung! Now, whimpering with the delirious certainty that death was upon him, he strove helplessly to rise. The cobra, detaching itself, coiled, weaved, and struck again.

Swiftly Operator 5 sprang up the basement stairs. His rush carried him quickly through the entrance, down the stoop. Wary eyes on the door of 1740—a door which hid a secret intrigue that would terrorize a nation if it became known—he sped across the street. At the opened entrance of his hideaway he glanced at his watch and saw that the hands pointed to thirteen minutes to twelve.

"Tim!" he called huskily. "After me, quick!"

With the boy running choppily at his side, he raced toward his roadster. Again, as he spurted the car away from the curb, he glanced at the gleaming dial of his watch.

Less than thirteen minutes for inescapable doom to descend upon twenty great leaders of the rearmament crusade!

OPERATOR 5 strode swiftly, Tim Donovan at his side, into the great War Department building in the heart of Washington. He had pressed his motor to the limit. In a conference room above the street the meeting of famed men was, at this very moment, he knew, in progress. Again his sharp eyes read the time.

Four minutes until midnight.

He sped up the stairs. Near the door which gave into the conference room two Intelligence men stood on guard. His sharp gesture moved them aside. He paused, hand on the knob, listening to a rumbling voice through the panels—the tones of the Chief of Staff addressing the meeting.

"The people must learn all the details, gentlemen! Our national existence depends upon their knowing that, while we remain almost defenseless, nations are arming all around us!"

"True!" a second voice boomed. "By God, gentlemen, our position is shameful! We're weaker than a dozen nations far smaller. Italy's able at this moment to mobilize an army twenty times larger than ours. This disgrace must end! I pledge myself to do everything in my power to—"

Operator 5 stepped briskly into the room, breathless Tim Donovan at his side. The eyes of twenty men turned upon him.

High officials of General Staff, famous state dignitaries, Senators, Representatives, civilians of prominence.

While they stared he strode directly to the head of the table, beside Major-General Falk.

"Gentlemen, you must abandon this room at once! If you stay here only a few moments longer you'll all be destroyed!"

General Falk demanded in a booming tone: "What the devil do you mean? We're to end this conference? It's vital to our program—"

"There will be no program unless you get out that door immediately!" Operator 5 snapped. "Look at that clock on the wall, gentlemen! It indicates two minutes to twelve. At exactly midnight an infernal machine—concealed in one of the cabinets in this room—will explode. For God's sake—"

"What's this!" the Chief of Staff protested. "An infernal machine—here? Impossible! How could anyone have planted it in these offices? Have you gone mad, young man? You interrupt us with a preposterous—"

"Listen!"

Operator 5's command stilled the Chief of Staff's heavy voice. A rustle of surprised movement faded away. Ears straining, Jimmy Christopher listened. At first there was only silence. Then, faintly—so faintly that it was scarcely audible at all—a sound. Regular, soft—and yet the pulsing of doom itself.

Tick, tick! Tick, tick!

"You hear it!" Operator 5 blurted. "Leave this room now, gentlemen! You have scarcely time to get out of the building before the second of midnight!"

NO MAN moved as he strode quickly along the green fronts of the file cabinets which walled the room. Again the rhythm became audible. *Tick, tick, tick!* It grew louder as he shot anxious glances at the spinning red hand of the electric clock on the wall. He paused abruptly, pressed his ear to one of the cabinets; straightened.

"It's in here—in this drawer!" His hand tugged hard at the handle. "The keys! Who has the keys of this file?"

The Secretary of the Joint Board jerked forward. "I have them! Here! God's sake—are you telling us the truth?"

"The absolute truth!" Operator 5 spun again to face the men "Can't you understand? There's sufficient explosive in this file to kill you all instantly! Get out—leave the building as fast as you can make it!"

His imperative voice brought a stampede of feet toward the door. Bewildered dignitaries, stricken suddenly with uncertainty, fear, crowded into the corridor.

Grimly Operator 5 turned as the Chief of Staff strode toward him. He glanced around to see that the room was almost emptied as he carefully slid the key into its socket.

"Leave, sir!" he implored General Falk. "I tell you there's no time—"

Slowly he slid the drawer open. The ticking became louder. Before his eyes lay the cunningly contrived mechanism of destruction. The entire rear of the drawer was filled with bundled sticks of dynamite from which electric wires ran through sealed metal tubes to a steel box. Inside the box the clock mechanism was ticking. The screws which held its metal lid in place had been covered with hard wax. Operator 5 glimpsed a strip of copper ribbon which came through a slot in the box, fastened to the tubes and the bottom of the drawer with solder.

"The box can't be opened in time!" Operator 5 exclaimed. "It can't even be lifted out of the drawer! A pull on that copper strip will trip the mechanism if we try it! It's impossible to stop this damnable device! Out of this room, sir—at once!"

Swiftly Jimmy Christopher slid the drawer shut. He whirled away; and the drawn paleness of his face spurred the Chief of Staff into action. General Falk loped desperately into the corridor behind his Secretary; and Tim Donovan poised on the sill, white-faced. Jimmy Christopher's glance shot to the electric wall-clock—and he saw the red hand spinning away the last few seconds until midnight!

He darted to the door and his lifted eyes glimpsed the outer panel as he drew it shut. On the polish there was a faint outline, scarcely visible—yet the keen eyes of Jimmy Christopher detected it now. He saw on the door of the conference room of the General Staff the same dread symbol that had marked the mural in the great International Hall during the Embassies Ball.

The scythe! The blade of the Grim Reaper!

"Fast, Tim!"

Operator 5 sped to the head of the stairs as the frantic boy raced after him. The two Intelligence men, who had been on guard, were poised uncertainly on the landing. Operator 5's sharp gesture forced them into a run. He bounded across the landing, poised to hurl himself down—and a thunderous roar went up through the great building. A deafening blast which jolted its very foundations.

Blinding flame sheeted high into the sky. The rumbling concussion shook beyond the building, sent great masses of masonry tumbling, writhing clouds of fumes pouring into the sky. The conference room of the General Staff was stripped to its framework in an instant. The force of the explosion hurled Operator 5 down the stairway and reeling, through clouds of blinding smoke.

"Jimmy, Jimmy!" Tim Donovan's voice rang frantically.

"Okay, Tim! Get below! Find your way out!"

Down broken steps Jimmy Christopher stumbled—over the bodies of two Intelligence men, crushed to death by a collapsing mass of stone.

On the lower floor of the building, far toward its front, the concussion had burst glass doors, and split walls and ceilings. Over spattered fragments of glass and plaster Operator 5 hurried into the outer air which was still clouded with fumes. Tim Donovan clung to his arm as he hurried toward the stunned group of men in the street—the men who had fled the room of doom at his command. Vast relief filled him as his eyes searched their faces. "Great God!" General Falk blurted in dismay. "The whole rear of the building is wrecked! Every one of us would have been killed!"

He broke off, struck wordless by the thought of the disaster.

Operator 5's answer came quietly: "An appalling thing, General Falk! But even worse—the great rearmament program would have been destroyed with you! That, sir, was the object of the mastermind who directed the planting of that bomb!"

OUTSIDE THE stricken building Operator 5 lingered until the crowd diminished, until startled officials of the State and War and Navy departments came hurrying to their shaken offices, until a small figure of a man appeared. Assistant Secretary of State Morten. Afterward he strode directly into the building with Tim Donovan at his side.

"Significant, Tim," he said softly as he approached the door of the Secretary of State's suite. "Morten was not in this building at midnight. He must know now that the twenty men escaped death. Surely he's learned of the affair at 1740. He's certain I'm responsible for this miscarriage of plans—and he's awaiting my report! Very well, then… he's going to get it right now."

He thrust open the door, strode to the Assistant Secretary's office, knocked. Morten's voice called "Come in!" He entered slowly, an enigmatic smile playing upon his lips as he faced the now feverish-eyed man on the far side of the desk.

A man who had set a trap of doom for him. A man who had planned his death, who knew that he alone grasped the full connection between the insidious espionage ring and the traitorous Assistant Secretary. A man who even yet gazed at him unflinchingly, coldly. His own wry smile deepened.

"You gave me orders to investigate Mayla Lazare, sir, and asked me to report to you."

Sibilantly Morten answered. "Yes."

"I recall also the orders of the Secretary of State that we of the Intelligence are forbidden to investigate the suspicion of treason within this department."

Tensely Morten answered. "Yes."

"I understand that to violate those orders, and the stipulations of Section 23, Code of Intelligence, would mean my instant dismissal from the service and, in addition, my imprisonment, perhaps for life."

Grimly Morten answered. "Yes!"

"If I have disobeyed orders and investigated that suspicion, if there is one in this Department who is working with the espionage ring, he will, because of his connection with it, know of my actions, will he not?"

"Yes!"

"But if he were to order me discharged from the Service on that basis he would, by doing so, betray his connection with the spy ring."

"Yes, yes!"

Operator 5's eyes blazed. "That being clearly understood, Mr. Assistant Secretary, I will now give you my report on the investigation of Mayla Lazare. It is this: there is no suggestion whatever of anything suspicious concerning her."

Slowly Randolph Morten straightened. His eyes shone. The twirk of Jimmy Christopher's lips tightened and he turned on his heel. He stepped out of the office and closed the door quietly: and as he turned away he knew that his battle of wits with the traitorous Assistant Secretary could continue to but one end:

Death.

Z-7 PEERED intently as Operator 5 briskly strode to the

chief's desk in the inner office of WDC-13, accompanied by Tim Donovan. He had come directly from the office of the Assistant Secretary of State. He had no opportunity to speak before Z-7 demanded stiffly:

"Operator 5, allow me to express my satisfaction over your discovery of the time-bomb in the General Staff's rooms—my gratitude that you succeeded in saving them from death. But it's necessary for me, here and now, to learn the source of your information concerning that bomb!"

Jimmy Christopher's eyes clouded. He stood motionless while the Washington chief went on.

"You were ordered off the Morten investigation. The Morten investigation links directly with the espionage ring which, you charge, is operating. The planting of that time-bomb is an act of that ring. If you learned of it, through investigating the ring, you were then indirectly investigating Morten and violating both my orders and those of the Secretary of State."

Still Operator 5 could not speak.

"If you have disobeyed those orders, Operator 5, I will have no choice but to dismiss you from the service on the spot!"

Across the desk the smouldering eyes of Z-7 and the darkening gaze of Operator 5 battled. The mounting tension was broken by the shrill ring of the desk telephone. Automatically Z-7 reached for it, his commanding stare still upon Jimmy Christopher.

"Well?" he demanded before he lifted the instrument. "What is your answer?"

"I learned of the time-bomb through following the orders of Assistant Secretary Morten to investigate Mayla Lazare, Chief."

Z-7 breathed a sigh. "Thank God for that! I want your written report."

Jimmy Christopher's mind was torn by a dilemma while Z-7 talked briskly over the wire. He realized that his report to the chief would conflict emphatically with the report he had already given Randolph Morten. The discrepancies would lead inevitably to questioning, to suspicion—perhaps to the dismissal which he now dreaded. He could reason no way out of his predicament before the Washington chief lowered the telephone with a thump, and snapped:

"T-6 reporting! I detailed him also to the job of trying to spot the secret organization of ex-Intelligence men. He's found their headquarters!" Z-7 gestured toward a pad on which he had just scribbled an address. "I'm going to look into that at once, myself. With your help, Operator 5, we can tonight take our first step toward crushing that organization!"

"I was about to add a second report, Chief," Jimmy Christopher answered. "I've also spotted the secret headquarters—the same address T-6 has given you. I suggest we put that place under watch at once."

"We'll do it now! Come with me, Operator 5!"

Z-7 strode grimly out of the office. Jimmy Christopher's eyes darkened with worry as he followed the chief, with Tim Donovan, out through the hidden elevator and the disguised doors. They reached the curb, where Operator 5's roadster was waiting. Jimmy Christopher took the wheel, and they started rapidly toward the address at which the Hidden Hundred had met in secret conclave.

"I am doubly determined to stamp out that organization now," Z-7 declared as he drew a flimsy from his leather case. "That action on the part of my old men amounts to treason. The organization, no matter what its object is, cannot be tolerated. The men who make it up are guilty of subversive actions under the Articles of War as well as the Code of Intelligence. Here, by the way, are the orders under which I am acting now!"

OPERATOR 5 read the flimsy as lights streaked past; and his lips grew grimly tight:

SPECIAL ORDERS... THE SECRET ORGANI-ZATION OF EX-INTELLIGENCE MEN MUST BE DESTROYED... EVERY RESOURCE OF THE INTEL-LIGENCE MUST BE MARSHALED TOWARD THIS END... THIS IS NOW OF THE UTMOST URGENCY AND THESE ORDERS TAKE PRECEDENCE OVER ALL OTHERS....

The signature was that of the Secretary of State.

Operator 5 said nothing as he sent the roadster winding into the remote district where the secret headquarters was hidden; and soon he drew to the curb near the address. As he shut off the motor he said quietly:

"It will not be easy, Chief, to execute these heavy penalties on men who once served us."

"It will not be easy, Operator 5, no. But our personal regrets can make no difference now. It must be done. That secret band must be destroyed. Its leaders must be punished to the fullest extent!"

They slipped from the car, and gazed at the sordid tenement from which Jimmy Christopher had seen the ex-service men emerge earlier that night. As they waited quietly, a dark figure drifted out of the shadows toward them. Intelligence Operator T-6 stopped alongside.

"I saw two men go in a moment ago, Chief," he reported. "Something new is in the wind!"

Grimly Z-7 directed: "We'll watch that place from different points. I'll take this corner. T-6, you watch from directly across the street. Operator 5, can you find a position at the rear? You, Tim, stick with him. Listen, carefully. We'll keep our eyes on it for exactly ten minutes. At the end of that time, we'll close in."

Quietly the three men checked their watches. Then they separated. Z-7 slipped into the shadows near the corner. T-6 walked briskly with Operator 5, then swung off and melted into the darkness of a doorway. With Tim Donovan, Operator 5 rounded the corner and walked along a board fence. He paused. Searched the gloom behind the suspicious building.

"Up, Tim!" he commanded.

He helped the boy over the fence, then vaulted it himself. They crept across a yard, cleared a second fence. Crouching in the darkness, Jimmy Christopher studied the rear of the house. His hand closed hard on the boy's arm.

"Get back in the corner, Tim. I'm going to take a position close to the door."

"Okay, Jimmy! Gee, it's going to be tough on those men when they're caught—and tough on the man who's leading them!"

Operator 5 nodded a grim agreement, and signaled the boy away. Tim Donovan crept along the fence, to the rear corner. An empty wooden crate offered him shelter, and he huddled behind it. Straining his eyes, he saw the faint figure of Operator 5 drifting along the fence, gliding closer to the house. In the deep shadow of the rear wall, Jimmy Christopher vanished. Tensely, Tim Donovan began a nerve-tingling wait.

As he peered through the empty gloom he sensed activity within the bleak walls of that house.

INSIDE THE black room at the front of the house stood two men who were wearing skull masks and skeleton gloves. They had entered the headquarters together; now they were awaiting the appearance of the secret leader. Soundlessness surrounded them long moments; but at last a rustling movement came out of the dark. Suddenly a dim light blinked on.

At a black table, shadowed in the glow, a third figure appeared, garbed also in the weird mask and skeleton gloves. His eyes shone keenly upon the two—the glittering eyes of the leader of the Hidden Hundred. He spoke in low, hushed tones:

"Comrades, I summoned you here for special orders, but they must be abandoned. At this moment, our headquarters is being surrounded by Z-7 and his men. They're planning to close in upon us in a few minutes. I want you to leave this place at once."

His claw-like hand reached to a black curtain at a front window. Pushing it gently aside, he pointed with his bony forefinger. The two masked men leaned forward peering along the direction indicated.

"In the doorway—there—T-6! Beyond, on the corner, Z-7. Behind the house—" He broke off abruptly to snap: "See? Already they're moving.... T-6 is coming toward the door! Don't wait a moment! You know the secret way out! Use it now!"

He stepped back, the drapes dropped together. Quickly the two men turned, strode out. Their commander shot one bony hand toward the light and clicked it out. Darkness filled the room. Again, as he listened to sounds beyond, by which he judged his two lieutenants were leaving by the secret way, he bent to peer through a crack of the curtain.

He saw T-6 mounting to the door. He turned quickly, to whisk himself through the black curtain covering the rear of the room—and at that instant a noise stopped him.

A latch clicked. A draft of cold air stirred the room. The man, T-6, was opening the front entrance! That door should have been firmly bolted—yet the step of T-6 was already sounding on the bare hallway floor!

A sharp movement ended in a thud. A ripping sound was followed by a louder thump, and a moan. Startled anew, the Hidden Hundred's leader jerked toward the connecting door. His hand shot to an electric switch, snapped it. Dim light, flashing in the corridor, revealed a sight that poised him rigid and motionless.

T-6 lay on the floor, inside the door—the hilt of a knife protruding from his chest above the heart. And above him, erect, trembling, stood the man who had driven the deadly blade—a man wearing the skull mask and skeleton gloves!

Instantly the leader of the Hidden Hundred leaped forward. The other snatched for a weapon; a gun twinkled in the light. The secret commander gripped the other's gun hand and reached to close the door. He shot home the bolt, whirled, and his clawed fingers caught at the eye-holes of the skull mask of the other man. Fabric ripped as he leaped back, and the features of T-6's killer were disclosed.

Thomas Zastrow!

A POWERFUL wrench, and the leader of the Hidden Hundred tore the weapon from Zastrow's numbed hand. The daring spy stood defiantly, back to the wall, as steps sounded in the street. They meant that Z-7 was hurrying to follow T-6 into the secret headquarters—and Zastrow's eyes gleamed in sudden triumph.

"Now!" he blurted hollowly. "Now you'll be hunted as the murderer of a man once your comrade!"

The master of the Hidden Hundred answered in cold fury. "You used the mask which belonged to D-4, Zastrow! You lied your way in on his written orders! You came from 1740, where he lies dead—a traitor to every cause he served, but an admirable man compared with you. You'll—"

A sharp knock sounded on the door.

The appalling tattoo paralyzed the leader of the Hidden Hundred for only an instant—but during that instant Zastrow lurched forward, jarred him against the wall, and drove out a telling blow which spun him back through the doorway, dazed.

As Zastrow leaped to the sill then, the front entrance shook violently. The old door was cracking under Z-7's determined impacts. The spy wheeled, dashed along the hall, charged at the rear door, jerked it open, sprang through....

Huddled in the shadows of the yard, Tim Donovan saw his lean figure silhouetted against dim light as he leaped forth. The Irish lad sprang up in consternation. As he ran, Zastrow darted toward the fence. The boy sped into the spy's path and flung himself into a tackle. His arms tightened around the lean body and he clung—until a savage blow to his temple dropped him flat.

Sobbing, he sprawled on the ground. Zastrow was clearing the fence even as he scrambled up again. Bewildered, he saw that the spy was fleeing into the street. His chubby hand groped into his hip pocket as he spurted toward the open rear door of the house. He dragged out a tiny automatic—a weapon he had special permission to carry—and shouldered through. He heard the crashing of Z-7's shoulder against the front entrance, saw a shadowed form hurrying toward him.

The leader of the Hidden Hundred, face masked and hands gloved uncannily, stopped short as Tim Donovan's weapon glinted.

"Go back!" the boy demanded.

Again the front entrance jarred, and screws screeched as they ripped from dry wood. The door was loosening; a few more blows would tear it down. The Irish lad's weapon leveled grimly as the eyes of the leader of the Hidden Hundred peered darkly at him.

"Don't move!"

"Tim!" For God's sake!"

THE BOY froze. He made no move as the masked leader reached swiftly for his gun. Too stunned to resist, he permitted his small automatic to be snatched away. He saw the leader whirl into the darkness behind the flight of steps. Dismayed, incredulous, he saw the marked gloves torn off, saw the weird mask slipped from the head of the master of the Hidden Hundred.

"Jimmy!" he blurted.

He peered aghast into Operator 5's drawn face. He was still peering as the front door shook once again and caved in, as Z-7 sprang through, his automatic glinting. He watched Z-7 take long strides along the hallway while Jimmy Christopher hastily and surreptitiously stuffed the mask and gloves into an inner pocket. He still stood frozen as Operator 5 stepped into the light, and cried:

"They've broken away, Chief. A secret door somewhere—they've escaped through that!"

A snarl broke from Z-7's lips. He tramped back along the hall and peered down at the still form on the floor—T-6, dead, a knife in his heart. In cold fury the Washington chief turned away. Jimmy Christopher stood quietly; Tim's widened eyes upon him, as Z-7 began a swift search of the secret headquarters on the upper floor.

"Jimmy!" the boy exclaimed again in horror.

"Easy, Tim," Operator 5 cautioned tensely. "You had to find out, someway, soon—but it's a secret which must be kept!"

"You know I'll stick with you no matter what happens, Jimmy."

"Thanks, old-timer! Be careful the chief—"

Z-7 rushed back down the stairs. Again he stopped, peering at the dead T-6. His black eyes smoldered furiously as Operator 5 and Tim Donovan came quietly to his side.

"Murdered!" he gritted. "Killed by the Hidden Hundred! Their leader is answerable for T-6's death! I'm going after that man now with all the power of the Intelligence! I'll never stop until I've got him for this! Nothing is going to keep me from making him pay the full penalty—nothing!"

The lines in Operator 5's drawn face deepened. He felt the frantic eyes of Tim Donovan upon him. There was silence between them—and in the light, the knife of a murderer glittering a promise of doom to Jimmy Christopher.

CHAPTER 9
THE SECRET POWER

THE HUGE room, the central agency of the far-flung Amalgamated Press, hummed and crackled with activity. In glass-enclosed booths telegraph instruments kept up a constant clatter, flashing news dispatches over a web of wires, to journals all over the United States. At a hundred desks typewriters clicked and reporters labored. Among them, working at fever heat, was the alert Diane Elliot.

Her darting fingers were typing the report of an exclusive interview she had had with Major James Mallard, retired—one of the staunchest proponents of the impending rearmament legislature. Mallard's statement was startling in the extreme, and in the heat of her excitement, Diane could picture it printed under scareheads from coast to coast.

"We cannot lie supinely helpless while active aggression is striking at us day by day in the West!"* her flashing keys printed.

"We must arm because we face grave danger. Economic war may easily become armed warfare at any moment—and when it does, we will lie defenseless before the foe unless we strengthen ourselves. We must arm now, or it will be too late!"

* AUTHOR's NOTE: A drive by Japan to crush down immigration barriers and open California to an Asiatic influx was revealed in San Francisco recently. Under the scheme, as disclosed by V.S. McClatchy, executive secretary of the California Joint Immigration Committee, Congress will be asked by influential allies of Japan in this country virtually to scrap the Exclusion Act of 1924 and grant Japan an annual immigration quota. The campaign to create public opinion along that line is already underway, and has been for months, McClatchy declared, with the purpose of compelling the present Congress to act. He said:

"Propaganda is being spread throughout Eastern newspapers and magazines. Unmistakable evidence of the campaign appears in interviews, articles and addresses by prominent Japanese officials and representatives, as well as by certain church dignitaries and commercial groups interested in securing Japan's favor."

Grant of an Oriental immigration quota, would be a "foot in the door," he added, opening the way to widespread Oriental immigration into the United States.

The excited girl carried her story across the clattering room to her superior, a man working at a large desk, eyes shadowed beneath a green shade. "I think its front page stuff!" she told him breathlessly.

He took the copy without speaking and began rapidly to read it. She returned to her desk and, mind still alert, resumed a task her interview had interrupted.

With sharp eyes she searched through the files of the most recent metropolitan newspapers. Her pencil made scrawling notes. Hurrying to a telephone she called the number of a house which was, in the lexicon of the U.S. Intelligence, designated Address Y—the home of John Christopher, father of Operator 5. She knew Jimmy had just flown to New York; and now his voice answered over the wire.

"I've been checking up, as you asked me to, Jimmy," she reported. "I've a dozen items here concerning Basil Van Praag. He's evidently traveling all over Europe on a long holiday. There have been reports on him almost every day. The latest is that he's at Monte Carlo."

Operator 5's voice came to her thoughtfully: "You have a dozen recent items—and yet Basil Van Praag has a reputation for shunning the limelight. Suddenly he's allowing notices about his movements to be printed in the world press. Thanks a lot, Di. My theory about him may amount to nothing, but—" His voice faded.

"Jimmy," the girl said anxiously, "I know you've come to town because of the great mass meeting to be held tomorrow night, but—I've a feeling that's not the only reason. You're running into serious danger, Jimmy—I know. Please be careful!"

His answer was grim. "I'll do my best, Di, but—I'm in this case to the end."

AS SHE hung up the receiver Diane wondered at his strange interest in the great Basil Van Praag. The name was a celebrated one. Van Praag was one of the wealthiest men in the world, one of the greatest newspaper owners. He virtually controlled the press throughout Europe, and it was rumored that his influence extended further, to across the sea. She looked at the latest item concerning the man, the item stating that he had stopped in Monte Carlo only the previous night, and her puzzlement grew.

Her gaze rose curiously as a man entered the humming office. She had seen this stranger appear several times daily for weeks; and always he conducted himself in a quiet, stealthily superior manner. Her curious questions as to who he was had elicited no information. Now she watched him walk directly to the desk of her chief.

He extended an envelope, then sank into a chair. Diane's chief read the letter, tore it to bits, and dropped it in a huge basket. He signaled a stenographer and dictated rapidly a few moments. When the stenographer withdrew with her notebook he summoned a subordinate and gave crisp directions. Soon Diane Elliot saw, placed in the hands of the messenger, a thick brown envelope.

Every day, at about this time, this same man had carried away a similar thick envelope. Diane believed its contents to be carbon copies of all the Amalgamated dispatches for the day. The messenger continued to wait—and she to watch.

Presently an office boy hurried in carrying to her a huge armload of newspapers fresh from the metropolitan presses. She selected several and returned to her desk. She was eager to read the report of her interview with Major Mallard.

But she did not find the report in the first. Startled, she looked in the others. Amazement filled her when she had completed her search. In none of the papers could she find the story which she had considered to be front-page news.

Impulsively she strode to the desk of her chief. He was signing a letter, and looked up as she said: "What's happened to my big story, Chief?"

"Killed," was the succinct answer. "Orders. This is for you. Don't ask any questions about it—I'm too busy."

DISMAYED, SHE read the letter he had handed to her. "I regret that your services to the Amalgamated Press are unsatisfactory and that we must dispense with them, effective at once. A check for one month's salary is attached."

Incredulously she peered at the green-shaded eyes—of her chief and blurted: "But—why? You know I'm a good reporter. Firing me out like this is—why, it's not fair!"

"Orders!" He snapped it without an upward glance. "Sorry, but that stands."

Diane Elliot returned to her desk and sat there stunned. She reread the letter of dismissal. She considered…. Yes, at last she had been caught in the strange power recently exerting itself in the Amalgamated headquarters. Reporters of undeniable ability had been ejected before her. A drastic shakeup was in progress—for unknown reasons. She felt grim anger—and a determination to learn who had ordered her discharged, and why.

Again studying the waiting messenger, she glanced at the newspapers. Another hint of the new power behind the Amalgamated came to her as she read:

GIGANTIC MASS MEETING TO PROTEST ARMS
BILLS TOMORROW NIGHT.
Famed Opponents of Militaristic Measures Rally Millions
Behind Cause.
Tomorrow night, in the great Times Square Garden, a tremendous meeting to protest the impending passage of the Arms Bills will be addressed by Assistant Secretary of State Randolph Morten. On the eve of the consideration of the munitions measures by Congress, the adherents of peaceful protectivism will strike a telling blow at the militarists whose program threatens to make the United States the suspect-imperialist of the world. The entire nation will back the sentiments of the great meeting.

Reading, Diane was appalled at what she knew to be deliberate garbling of the facts. The huge meeting scheduled for the next evening was not alone a protest; it was to be a debate at which the proponents of the defense program would also speak. Yet this was not mentioned. This item would cause thousands to crowd into the great hall under false impressions—it would bring opponents of the measure out in numbers to overwhelm those who favored the Arms Bills. The girl compared this report with another in a different paper and noted discrepancies which could mean only one thing—deliberate, subversive propaganda!

Another item fascinated her as she continued to watch the mysterious messenger:

PRESIDENTIAL POLL REVEALS DEADLOCK IN CONGRESS ON ARMS MEASURES!

Personal Inquiry by Chief Executive Shows Senators and Representatives Evenly Divided—People Must Decide.

What promises to be a complete deadlock, which can be broken only by the will of the people, was disclosed in a presidential statement late today. On the eve of the extraordinary session of Congress, called for special consideration of the Arms Bills, the President declared that the outcome will be impossible to foresee until the people themselves rise to make the momentous decision.

The great mass meeting in New York tomorrow night is expected to be the deciding factor. The President believes that, as the nation responds to this meeting, Congress will reflect their attitude. He expressed fear that the Arms Measures will be defeated and that the United States will be doomed to continued unarmed helplessness....

DIANE'S EYES brightened as her chief placed a second brown envelope in the hands of the waiting messenger. The messenger rose at once—carrying, she felt sure, the final, complete copies of the day's dispatches—and strode out. Quickly the girl followed, assuming a casual manner as she stepped into the elevator cage with the messenger. She noted the hard lines of his face, the contemptuous cast of his eyes.

When he reached the street and signaled a cab, she summoned another. The first turned into the stream of traffic as she slipped a banknote into the hand of her own driver. "Don't let that taxi get out of sight!" she ordered. Eyes alert, she settled back. The chase began.

Through heavy traffic, the two taxis wound northward. At Seventy-Second Street the one ahead turned west, turned again on Riverside Drive. Traveling more rapidly, Diane's kept close behind. Soon the first drew to the curb and the hard-faced man alighted. Diane hurried from her taxi as he entered a huge, imposing apartment building. Daringly, she stepped into the lobby directly behind him, even more daringly entered the same elevator cab.

His eyes searched her face; hers were a challenge. She did not speak and the cab slid upward until a command from the messenger stopped it. He strode into a hallway hung with fine oil-paintings, and Diane promptly followed. Startled, he paused, scanned her face anew; then, turning without speaking, he strode through a door.

She stepped to it, put a hand to the knob, and listened. She heard a voice say, "The day's dispatches, sir." Another answered "Good! That's all," and steps sounded. When another inner door closed, she opened the one she faced. Chin lifted, eyes bright, she strode straight into the huge, luxuriously furnished library—straight to the desk upon which the two thick brown envelopes now rested.

The man behind the desk rose in astonishment. His face was a strange one to her—sharp, shrewd, merciless. The eyes flashed with dangerous lights as he peered at her. But coldly, without fear, she gazed back as she said:

"I'm Diane Elliot. I've just been discharged by the Amalgamated Press. I don't know who you are or what influence you have there—but I demand to know why I was fired!"

The man at the desk simulated astonishment. "My dear young lady," he said icily, "I don't know what you're talking about. I never heard of you. The Amalgamated Press means nothing to me. This is a private home. You've made a mistake."

She insisted. "I want to know why I was fired—and who sent the orders your messenger carried."

He bristled. "Are you mad? You can't invade a private home in this manner. If you don't leave at once, I'll have you taken out!"

Her eyes blazed; but uncertainty filled her. She hesitated, nervously fingering her purse. The man touched a button; the door behind the girl opened, and a servant entered. "This young lady is leaving," the man at the desk said.

Diane hesitated; then, because she realized the impetuosity of her move, because no other response was possible, she left the library.

BEWILDERED, SHE heard the voice of the man at the desk speaking softly as she stepped into the hall. She waited for the elevator a long moment. As she stepped through the opened grille, her suspicions returned. She was alone in the cab with the attendant until it paused at a lower level. Then the grille opened once more and a young woman stepped in. At sight of her Diane Elliot's nerves gave a jump. The woman was Mayla Lazare!

Diane's mind raced, as the car descended. She realized now that a telephone message from the library above had ordered a woman spy after her. She was to be shadowed and watched. A tingling sense of danger filled her as she felt the eyes of the Lazare woman coldly studying her. She pretended not to notice; and when the cab opened at the street level she stepped out with a quickly formed plan of action in mind.

At the curb she called a cab. A backward glance showed Mayla Lazare walking away. When she stepped into the taxi, she saw the woman spy turn quickly and signal another. Grim satisfaction came to Diane; the move verified her suspicions. Mayla Lazare was trailing her! Now, deliberately, she gave her driver an address in the East Forties of Manhattan—the number of the house in which Operator 5's father lived.

When, at last, her cab turned toward its destination, she quickly told the driver to stop, slipped out, paid him, and began walking toward the house designated Address Y. She sensed, without looking, that Mayla Lazare's cab had also stopped; that the woman was following on foot now. She moved close to the buildings; turned to a doorway below the sidewalk level next to Address Y.

Her hand eased into her purse and lifted, gripping the butt of a tiny automatic. She heard the quick steps of Mayla Lazare drawing near. The dark figure of the woman appeared; and at once Diane Elliot stepped forward. When she paused, her face was within inches of the woman spy's; her gun was pressing into the other's body.

The woman jerked tight; and Diane said softly: "You wish to learn where I am going? I'll tell you. It is directly next door. And you're going in with me!"

Mayla Lazare hesitated. Her dark eyes flashed a threat. But still Diane's gun pressed hard. She shifted so that its pressure started the other forward. Coldly she marched the now furious woman spy to the door of Address Y. With a key she unlocked the way. Again she forced her captive forward, up a flight of stairs, through the door of a comfortable, warm living-room. At their entrance a startled voice said:

"Diane!"

John Christopher, father of Operator 5, once designated Operator Q-6 in the U.S. Intelligence, stared astounded. He was a mild-mannered man whose face was gaunt yet kindly. During his service he had suffered a serious wound which had incapacitated him. Two bullets lay so close to his heart that no surgeon dared operate to remove them; they constantly threatened John Christopher with death. Proud of his son, he relived his own service in the other's exploits.

"Isn't Jimmy here?" Diane asked breathlessly.

"No! He's at MW. Who is this woman?"

"I'm going to find out," Diane declared ringingly, "just who she is and what she's doing!"

AGAIN, WHILE Mayla Lazare's beautiful face worked with anger, Diane's gun forced the spy forward into an adjoining bedroom. Carefully transferring her tiny automatic to

John Christopher, and while the astounded man kept the spy covered, she snatched curtain-cords from the windows. When she completed her task the woman spy lay bound helpless on the bed. Diane Elliot laughed softly.

Quickly she turned from the room and closed the door. John Christopher had followed her out and now stared at her in bewilderment. "What does this mean, Di? Is this woman connected—"

"With the espionage ring Jimmy's told us about? Yes!" The girl answered excitedly. "She's working with Morten, and scores of others, under a leader so powerful he absolutely controls the Amalgamated. She's in the thick of it—and I'm going to learn exactly in what way!"

"Look here!" ex-Operator Q-6 protested. "If you do that you'll be violating the civilian clause of Section 23 of the Code of Intelligence! You know the penalty for that, Di—imprisonment, perhaps for life! You can't run that risk!"

"I'm going to run it," the girl exclaimed firmly. "But please don't tell Jimmy. He mustn't know—he'd only try to stop me, and I'm simply not going to let myself be stopped now. I want to keep that woman a prisoner here while I—"

Diane broke off, her eyes shining with determination. Suddenly she turned and entered the rear rooms where lay the workshop of Operator 5. They were filled with strange apparatus, equipped as a combination radio, chemical and mechanical laboratory.

From a chest of drawers she quickly removed two metal boxes. Then, chin lifted defiantly, she carried them out, turned to the door of the room in which Mayla Lazare lay bound, and strode inside.

John Christopher heard a bolt click into its socket; and he stared at the panels in wondering dismay.

SECRET INTELLIGENCE Headquarters MW, in New York, had not existed a month before and in another month it would vanish without a trace. Now it was carefully housed in a huge building in the upper city which, apparently, was one of many warehouses in the district. Dark, lonesome, its walls hid humming activity.

On an upper floor a suite of rooms housed the files, the communications station, the offices of the subheadquarters. That of Z-7 was located far back in the labyrinth of doors and walls. In it now stood Operator 5 and Tim Donovan, facing the Washington chief. Z-7 had followed them by plane from Washington; his orders had summoned Jimmy Christopher. His eyes smoldered, his voice became edged, as he spoke. "I am absolutely positive," he declared, "that the Hidden Hundred has shifted operations to this city. All our ex-Intelligence men have vanished from Washington; have come here. I must know why. I'm still bound by the orders of the Secretary of State to do everything possible to crush that subversive organization out of existence!"

"Perhaps they're in New York, Chief," Jimmy Christopher answered, "because the activities of the espionage ring have also shifted to this city—because of the huge mass meeting tomorrow night."

"With that we are not concerned!" Z-7 snapped. "Our orders

161

to keep hands off on that ring still stand. Above everything else, the Hidden Hundred must be destroyed!"

Operator 5's eyes darkened. "Chief, must our hands remained tied when the nation faces such a crisis? The forces, pro and con, on the Armament Bills are now evenly balanced. No man can predict which way Congress will be forced to vote. Upon that vote depends the destiny of the United States. The vote, in turn, depends upon the response of the people to the mass meeting tomorrow night. Isn't it a certainty that the espionage ring will seize upon that opportunity to decide the issue somehow? For God's sake, can't we prepare ourselves against that emergency?"

"Without the approval of the Secretary of State, we cannot!"

"The Hidden Hundred is acting in the interests of the nation—acting without the restrictions of hide-bound rules, doing what we are unable to do—and yet you order them destroyed!"

"Because my chief demands it—yes!"

"Very well, Z-7," Operator 5 answered tensely. "The Intelligence, tomorrow night, will officially do nothing more than post guards at Times Square Garden—nothing more than that, while a crisis cries for action! I thank God the Hidden Hundred are at work!"

Grimly Jimmy Christopher turned on his heel and strode to the door. As he opened it, a sharp word from Z-7 stopped him. The Washington chief's black eyes were shining dangerously. His voice was edged, threatening, as he said:

"I've a growing suspicion of the identity of the leader of the

Hidden Hundred. If my suspicion is correct—if I find proof to back me up—be certain I'll act swiftly and drastically, my boy!"

The words chilled Operator 5. He forced a slow smile while Tim Donovan's eyes clung anxiously to his face. Quietly he answered:

"I know you will. You can do nothing else. I understand that fully."

He stepped out and Tim Donovan walked quickly at his side. They stepped into an Intelligence machine waiting at the curb. The Irish lad's hot hand sought Operator 5's.

"Jimmy—the chief suspects you! If he ever finds proof—gee, it'll be the end of you!"

"It will, Tim," Operator 5 answered gravely. "There's no possible doubt of that!"

HIS FINGERS gripped the wheel tensely as he drove south. He did not speak as he followed Fifth Avenue along Central Park, then turned east in the Sixties. Slowing, he glanced at the front of a staid apartment house. Then his searching glance swept the street. When he turned the far corner his lips pressed tightly, and he said in a whisper too low even for Tim's ears:

"Spies are watching for Huntley Walsh and Carleton Victor."

He drove across the city quickly, turning again so that he soon passed the great hall in which the mass meeting was scheduled to be held the next night. Quietly he gave orders to the Irish lad.

"This place is supposed to be empty tonight, Tim, but I want you to keep watch on it. The usual preparations have already been made for the meeting. Keep your eyes sharp for anything suspicious—and wait for me near the entrance."

163

The boy left the car and sauntered away as Operator 5 again turned east. Crossing town once more he pulled to a curb in the East Forties, in front of the home of his father. His searching glance probed the street shadows as he opened the lock with a key. He bounded up the stairs, strode into the living-room—and stopped short in amazement.

One of the connecting doors opened as he entered. Through it a young woman stepped. A young woman with a beautiful face of foreign cast—but a face which sent a chill through him.

"Mayla Lazare!"

The young woman stood peering at him intently. And then a warm smile changed the coldness of her beauty. "I guess I've done a pretty good job of it, then," she said.

"Di!" Operator 5 exclaimed. He stepped forward, peering incredulously. "It isn't possible!"

"Jimmy—you mustn't try to stop me!" Again Diane's voice came from the lips of Mayla Lazare. "I have a lead I've got to follow. I used your makeup kit—and I'm going now. I've a feeling this is going to lead straight to the master mind behind the espionage ring!"

"Good Lord, Di!"

Ex-Operator Q-6 stepped from an adjoining room and Jimmy Christopher greeted him absently. He strode to the door from which the disguised girl had stepped. Opening it, he saw a second surprising sight. A young woman bound hand and foot on the bed, divested of her outer clothing, effectively gagged. The real Mayla Lazare's dark eyes blazed hatred at him.

He returned to the living-room to see John Christopher alone in it. Diane's footfalls were sounding quickly on the steps.

"Di!" he called anxiously. Hurrying after her, he saw the entrance close. He sprang, opened it. But nowhere on the street did he see the girl. Unconquerably determined, she was hastening to follow the lead she had discovered—a lead promising unknown dangers.

As he returned to the living-room John Christopher exclaimed: "There's no stopping her now, Jimmy! She searched the woman's purse and found a typewritten order in code. She worked it out—a message giving Mayla Lazare an appointment with an unknown man at a secret headquarters. God knows what she's heading into, Jimmy!"

OPERATOR 5'S eyes darkened with anxiety. Added explanations from his father only increased the dread suddenly weighing his heart.

"There's nothing to do now but let her follow it through, Dad!" he decided.

"I'm leaving at once, but please stay here. Diane may phone in a report. Mayla Lazare must be watched. And—"

Jimmy Christopher reached for the telephone and hesitated, while ex-Operator Q-6 said quietly: "Son, I realize the odds you're up against—and the danger the country is facing. I've been studying our situation in the west and I know economic strife there is becoming more and more bitter. That in fact, is where our real danger lies.* It would be fatal not to arm ourselves against the threat. That's why I've telegraphed to the Secretary of State and requested that I be reinstated in the Intelligence."

"You've done that, Dad? Even knowing the restrictions we work under now—even knowing the exertion might be—too much for you?"

"I can't stand idly by and do nothing in this emergency, Jimmy," John Christopher answered. "No matter if it costs me my life, I want to go back into active service. I'm expecting word from the Secretary at any time. I'm expecting him to accept me."

Operator 5's eyes lighted. "I hope he does, Dad. I'll be proud

---

* AUTHOR'S NOTE: A world famous newspaper correspondent, verifying recent reports that Japan has kept her munitions factories going day and night, and has been accumulating reserves of oil, iron, tin and other raw materials needed for war purposes, pointed out that with her withdrawal from the League of Nations and her scrapping of the Far Eastern Naval Limitations treaties, Japan gained a free hand to arm and at the same time almost completely isolate herself from the rest of the world. This correspondent pointed out that Japan is staking her future on a hazardous gamble to make herself mistress of the Orient. Her success will mean, he declared, bringing half the population of the globe directly or indirectly under her empirical control. While Japan is expending nearly half her huge national budget on her army and navy, and while her people are being taxed to the utmost, the world watches with dismay.

"All Western powers fear for their world trade which, by a combination of modern chain production, government subsidies, cheap labor and aggressive business methods, Japan is grabbing at an alarming rate."

to be working with you again." He lifted the telephone, eyes narrowed in thought. Quietly he called a number.

Many blocks away, in a sumptuous apartment, a bell purred in the home of the noted photo-portraitist, Carleton Victor. Victor maintained impressive studios on Fifth Avenue; his reputation was such that the most outstanding personages in the world considered it an honor to sit before his lens. A portrait signed with Victor's name was a credential of high importance. Here, in this exquisitely furnished apartment, he lived quietly and alone with his estimable Crowe.

Crowe, gentleman's gentleman extraordinary, answered the summons of the telephone. With pride and dignity he announced: "The home of Carleton Victor."

"Good evening, Crowe," a familiar voice said over the line.

"Good evening, Mr. Victor!" The manservant glanced aside at a spotless table, set with gleaming crystal and glittering silver. Nightly Crowe prepared an exquisite dinner for Victor; frequently he suffered the keenest disappointment when his master did not appear to partake of his cookery; yet a hundred disappointments could not have led the efficient Crowe to neglect the preparations. "You will not dine at home tonight, sir?" he inquired.

Jimmy Christopher's voice answered: "No, Crowe. I'm very busy."

Crowe did not suspect that the identity of Carleton Victor was a convenient mask for the activities of Operator 5. Nor did any of the notables who sat before the celebrated photographer's lens dream of it. When he entered these rooms, Operator 5 became Carleton Victor, artist of the camera; and to Crowe his word was higher than the law.

"Very good, sir."

"But," Carleton Victor continued, "there is something I wish you to do for me, Crowe. In my study you'll find my camera case. The large, black one, Crowe. I need it for a special task tonight. Please carry it directly up the avenue toward the Vandervoort Hotel. If I don't meet you on the way, I'll meet you in the lobby. Be very careful of the case, Crowe—and leave at once."

"Very good, sir."

Crowe promptly slipped into his topcoat, wrapped a muffler around his chin, fitted a square derby on his head; and in the study he took into his careful hand the Morocco-leather camera-case of the famous Mr. Victor. Carrying it gingerly as though all the precious things in the world were contained in it, he left the apartment, then the building, and began walking briskly according to his master's directions.

TO REACH the Vandervoort Hotel it was necessary for Crowe to turn east. He walked along the quiet cross-street, his pointed nose lifted with cool dignity, as if he were conscious of nothing but the extreme care Mr. Victor's equipment demanded. He scarcely saw a black figure slip from a doorway as he passed it. He was first aware of the presence when he felt something touch his back and heard a muffled command:

"Give me that case!"

He turned, frowning—and his face went white. He was peering at an apparition the like of which he had never seen before. A being garbed in well made clothing, wearing a hat—indeed, in all respects having the appearance of a normal man—with two startling exceptions. First, the figure's head was not a head but fleshless skull! Second, the hands were not hands but bony claws! What was finally and even more disturbing to the estimable Crowe, one of those skeleton hands was leveling an automatic at him.

Crowe blurted. "I beg your pardon?"

"Drop that case!"

The manservant blinked. In any emergency his poise remained unshaken, but the present situation put a telling strain on it. His hand on the case handle tightened. He answered, as his nose twitched nervously:

"I'm carrying out an important mission, sir, if I may say so. This case belongs to Mr. Carleton Victor and I'm quite sure he wouldn't wish me to—"

"Drop it! Let it go or you'll die where you stand!"

The tip of Crowe's pointed nose grew red with consternation. The ring of the living skeleton's voice brooked no disobedience. The glint of the eyes in the bony sockets were dark threats. The pressure of the gun over his heart was disconcerting in the extreme. Indignantly Crowe followed instructions—except that he did not drop the case. He lowered it with the greatest care.

"Turn around! Walk slowly! Don't look back!"

Trembling with repressed fury Crowe complied. He turned. He walked slowly. He did not look back. To a man accustomed to executing orders he found these instructions singularly difficult to execute, but he strove mightily—remembering the gun. When he reached the corner he stepped past; then, daring the danger, he glanced back. The street was empty. The skeleton figure and the case of Carleton Victor were gone.

Filled with dismay now, Crowe hurriedly retraced his steps. In no shadow did he find the weird robber. Frantic with anxiety, he hurried on, to the marquee of the Vandervoort. He stepped into the luxurious foyer, trembling with profound concern, and a sigh of relief escaped him as he glimpsed Carleton Victor sitting comfortably in an easy chair, casually smoking an imported cigarette.

"Sir!" he exclaimed under his breath as Victor rose. "I've been robbed! Your case has been stolen! I could not prevent it, Mr. Victor. My life was threatened!"

Carleton Victor frowned sharply. "What's that, Crowe? You've lost my case? A pretty confession to make! Don't you realize—?"

"But I was overwhelmed, sir! The gent—the thing—the—I don't know *what* it was that robbed me, sir, but he—it—threatened to murder me on the spot, if I may say so, sir!" Crowe straightened and his face took on the expression of a martyr. "I beg your pardon, sir. I realize now that I should have refused, even in the face of that. You entrusted me with an important mission and I have failed. There is nothing left for me to do, sir, but offer my resignation."

"Nonsense!" Carleton Victor said. "I can get another camera, but in this world there's not another manservant like you, Crowe. But don't stand there looking like someone about to be burned at the stake. Get busy! Notify the police!"

"Yes, sir!" Crowe blurted.

"And then return to the apartment, Crowe. I recommend also, that you take something to quiet your nerves."

"Very good, sir!" The dismayed manservant hurried in the direction of an illuminated arrow pointing the way to telephone booths. A chuckle passed Carleton Victor's lips. He crossed the lobby to the hat-check stand, proffered the very blonde girl there a brass check. In exchange for it he received a black morocco-leather camera case—the case the skeleton figure had wrested from Crowe.

SMILING, HE left the Vandervoort, signaled a cab, which presently carried him westward. He opened the case and checked its contents—strange devices, carefully stored in compartments. They were of no avail to Carleton Victor in the making of photographs; they were, however, of vital importance to the operations of Operator 5 and the leader of the Hidden Hundred.

His subterfuge had been necessary because of his certainty that Victor's apartment was being watched; because the transference of this case from Victor to the captain of the Hidden Hundred must be covered.

He left the cab in front of Times Square garden. Near the foyer Tim Donovan was waiting. The boy sauntered to his side and spoke without moving his lips, while apparently merely waiting for a chance to earn a tip from the well-dressed gentleman, for carrying his case.

"There're workmen in there, Jimmy. Some of them look suspicious. All the decorations are up, and these men are doing something special—I don't know what."

Operator 5 passed a coin to the boy and gave him the case.

"Be careful of that, young man." Then, in a lower tone: "We're going to take a look inside, Tim. Follow me."

He rounded the corner, the Irish lad carrying the case at his side. Near one of the entrances he paused. He found it locked; but, as if accustomed to entering this building in this manner, he drew out his pack of master keys. Drawing the bolt was not difficult. He entered a cement vestibule from which stairs rose. With the boy still at his side, he climbed them.

Quietly he stepped onto a balcony. Before him lay the vast auditorium—huge enough for three-ring circuses, horse shows, rodeos, polo matches. Pilot lights gleamed upon the special speaker's platform erected and decorated with tri-colored bunting; the gleam cast the shadows of men here and there on the walls.

They were working behind the arena seats, with wire and black bundles. Operator 5 studied their strange actions, then opened his case and removed a pair of binoculars. The powerful lenses enabled him to examine the operations of the men in detail. He saw that they were opening ventilators, heat grilles, hose boxes. In these spaces they were placing the black bundles. From the bundles thin insulated wires trailed. The wires were being concealed.

Operator 5's eyes sharpened through the binoculars. His face was grave when he lowered the glasses.

From his case he removed a small metal box. To pin-jacks in its sides he attached ear-phones and a super-sensitive microphone. Other leads connected the device with powerful but small batteries connected in the case. He crouched, affixed the phones to his ears, pressed the rubber-mounted microphone to the cement floor, and slowly turned a black knob.

Long moments he remained motionless except for the flexing of his fingers on the knob. When he rose his seriousness was even more marked. He quickly returned the instrument to his case. Gloom covered him as he retraced his steps. Tim strode with him down the stairs, together they stepped outside the entrance. There Operator 5 paused, his eyes glinting darkly.

"What is it, Jimmy?" The Irish lad spoke anxiously.

OPERATOR 5 answered slowly. "Those men are installing something which is to be actuated electrically. They're working alone, under orders, but secretly. When they finish, there will be no sign of their work. As for the other preparations—

"That device I used, Tim, is an extremely sensitive and powerful sound-amplifying apparatus. It magnifies any noises it picks up millions of times. Listening through it, I heard impulses reverberating through the building. The men I've already mentioned weren't making them. They would be inaudible by any other means. It was the sound of digging—of other men beneath the building, making some sort of an excavation."

"Gee, Jimmy! Why would anyone be doing that?"

Operator 5 answered tersely: "I want you to try to find out, Tim. I have a strong suspicion, but it must be verified. Try to learn what's up—but don't let yourself be seen. Stay here until you find out. Wait until I come back, even if it's not until tomorrow night. If what I suspect is true, it's a matter of life and death—of the lives and deaths of thousands!"

Operator 5 turned briskly and strode away, leaving the boy

staring in dismay. At the corner he signaled a cab. His orders sent it across town, into the East Forties. He alighted before Address Y and entered briskly. He stepped into the living room to find his father seated dejectedly in a chair, lost in a spell of painful dejection, holding a telegram loosely in one hand.

"Dad! What's wrong?"

Ex-Operator Q-6 looked up haggardly. "Hello, Jimmy." He spoke wanly. "I—I've just heard from the Secretary of State. He's refused to—to readmit me to the Service."

Grimness tightened Jimmy Christopher's lips as he took the telegram from his father's fingers. He read the terse, cold message and his eyes blazed:

IMPOSSIBLE DUE TO YOUR AGE AND PHYSICAL CONDITION TO GRANT YOUR REQUEST.

"Brutal!" Jimmy Christopher exclaimed. "Dad, you're the best man who ever worked in the Service. You can outshine any one of us even today. Z-7 would be delighted to welcome you back, but—"

John Christopher rose. "In spite of the Secretary's decision, I'm going to help all I can. I want to work with you, Jimmy, unofficially. If you'll let me serve at your side—"

Quietly Operator 5 answered: "In the crisis facing this country now, we need men like you, Dad."

He strode to the door of the room in which he had last seen Mayla Lazare lying bound, a prisoner. He twisted the knob and looked in.

A freezing coldness flowed through his veins. The shock of

surprise held him motionless. He peered at the rumpled bed, at a closet standing open showing the disarrayed dresses of Diane Elliot, at a window yawning into the court. He snapped back, blurted in dismay:

"Dad! Mayla Lazare's broken loose! She's gone!"

CHAPTER 10
POWER BEHIND POWER

IN THE lobby of the huge apartment building on River-side Drive, the young woman who was, to all appearances, Mayla Lazare, raised her gloved hand to the elevator button. She waited with tense nerves until the elevator grille slid open. Diane stepped into the cab; her heart beat fast as the cage lifted her toward the dangerous place above.

She had hurried directly here from Address Y; had watched the building carefully through long minutes. The cryptic type-written orders in Mayla Lazare's purse had specified the hour of a secret appointment; that hour was now at hand.

The cab stopped, and she stepped out. A short time ago, as Diane Elliot, she had left this mysterious suite of rooms. Now, as Mayla Lazare, she entered the vestibule while the eyes of a sharp-faced manservant studied her. He opened another door and she strode into the library to which the strange brown enve-lopes had been brought from the Amalgamated's central office. Behind the desk the same keen-eyed man was sitting. He turned a searching gaze her way.

"I am ready," Diane Elliot said.

The man at the desk rose, smiling slowly. Diane's heart quickened again with the thought that his sharp gaze was penetrating her disguise. She waited an interminable, torturous minute before he asked: "Your orders?" She took the coded slip from her purse and handed it into his thin fingers. He studied it, peered at her again, and said quietly:

"Are you unwell? You seem a bit—changed."

"I am quite well," the startled girl answered. "I—I don't like to be late."

"No. Follow me."

He opened a door and she passed through. He led her to the wall, to a huge mural. His hand touched one golden ornament of its frame. Hidden machinery whirred; the great painting slid aside. Behind it showed the waiting cab of a small elevator. The man urged her forward. As she stepped into it—she felt that she was walking into a trap.

The painting slid back into place, closing her in the small cubicle. Machinery whirred. Immediately the small cab began to rise. The canvas of the painting slid downward; blank wall took its place. For a long moment she felt herself lifted; then, gently, the cab clicked to a stop.

The panel in front of her parted. She stepped through, into a small room luxuriously furnished. The tapestries on its walls looked rare and priceless; the several oils were genuine old masters. In this silent room, far above the Drive, she stood tensed and waiting until a door opened quietly and a man stepped forward.

His face was cadaverous, his eyes dead: he bowed like an

automaton and held the way open for her. She passed him with a shudder, and entered a spacious library beyond. The richness of this room also was evident at a glance. Shelves loaded with rare volumes. Ming vases, more genuine old masters, other Gobelin tapestries. Yet, fascinating as the decorations were to one who appreciated their pricelessness, it was the man in the room who drew Diane Elliot's eyes magnetically.

He was seated behind a huge, carved, flat-topped desk. His forehead was high, his eyes shadowed deeply by white brows. His white Vandyke was trimmed to a sharp point. His was a face of power—a face she recognized instantly. This man was Basil Van Praag.

THE GREAT newspaper publisher rose slowly, smiling. His graceful gesture invited her to a chair. She went to it attempting desperately to preserve her casual manner. She returned his smile, faced him across the polished desk. In the glow of the lamp they studied each other in silence.

"It's a long time, Mayla," he said quietly, "since we've seen each other."

Diane forced herself to answer: "A long time. Too long."

"Yes, too long. I am delighted to see you again. You've distinguished yourself admirably in the cause, my dear. You're one of a rare few who have faced me here. You see, I trust you completely—I rely upon your shrewdness and your intelligence."

"I'm grateful."

"No one but you and Zastrow and Raneo know I'm in the United States. My subordinates in Europe have been publishing false notices in my papers, following me on an imaginary trip along the Riviera. Perhaps they deceived you too, Mayla. No matter. I've a most important mission to place in your very capable hands."

"I'll do my best."

"Of course. There is, my dear, an organization working under cover against us. It's made up of daring men—it's powerful! The United States Intelligence we do not fear, but this organization threatens us. It's known as the Hidden Hundred."

Diane tensely nodded.

"Its members are made up of ex-Intelligence men who boldly defy every law in their purpose to serve the nation which has renounced them. They're not bound by any regulations or restrictions. They stop at nothing to fulfill their purpose. That purpose is to destroy our organization—to learn my identity, as the commander, and destroy me. Now we must destroy it!"

Diane Elliot whispered in fascination: "Yes!"

"You—you'll enable us to do that, Mayla! It's your task to identify the leader of the Hidden Hundred. We don't know who he is, but you must learn. You must tear away the cloak of mystery that conceals him—single him out so he can be removed, once and for all. Your task can terminate in only one way—by the death of the leader of the Hidden Hundred."

A buzz sounded like a period to the man's softly spoken yet menacing statement. He reached for his desk telephone, lifted it, listened without speaking. His deeply shadowed eyes widened. His blue-veined hand went white. Without having uttered a syllable, he slowly returned the instrument to its standard. His tension vanished; he looked again at Diane Elliot—and smiled.

178

"One moment, my dear," he said in a whisper. "I have a visitor whom you must meet."

He rose and went to the door. Diane heard a faint grinding sound; the secret elevator rising. She heard the mechanism part the panel, and quick, light steps come toward the door. In the light a young woman appeared—a woman who stopped on the sill, peering at her with eyes cold and triumphant, red lips curved mockingly.

The newcomer was Mayla Lazare.

AS ANOTHER night rolled across the United States like a black, uncurling carpet the voice of a radio announcer spoke over a broadcasting network reaching from coast to coast; by short-wave his words traveled around the world.

"Ladies and gentlemen of the radio audience, we are speaking to you from the great Times Square Garden, in New York City. Tonight the tremendous mass meeting to decide the fate of the Rearmament Bills is gathering. The speaking will not begin for almost an hour, but the doors are open and thousands are crowding to their seats. In the streets outside, thousands more are clamoring for admittance. All New York is centering upon this building tonight; all the world is looking at this spot. For, on this platform, within a few hours, the fate of a nation will be decided."

From a hundred antennae, echoing through millions of radio receivers, the hubbub of the crowd could be heard—the voices and footfalls of the thousands clambering into the arena and the balconies of the great Times Square Garden.

"Late this afternoon," the announcer continued, "the Presi-

179

dent repeated his poll of Congress. The deadlock remains unbroken. The representatives of the people have forgotten party alliances and personal opinions in their endeavor to decide this momentous issue fairly. Only the voice of the people of the United States can finally decide it now. Their response to tonight's great demonstration cannot be foreseen at this moment—but means have been provided so that the whole people may speak and be heard here tonight."

Far across the Atlantic and the Pacific, the dignitaries of foreign governments listened to the words. In the Far East, sunlight blazed; in Europe it was past midnight of the previous day; but time was forgotten as the statesmen of the world prepared to wait until the American people had voiced their decision on an issue which affected the military programs of the entire world.

"In this building, ladies and gentlemen," the announcer explained, "a tremendous bank of telephone switchboards has been installed, and a gigantic assembly of teletype machines. A huge force of operators is prepared to receive messages from all over the nation. Every man and woman is urged to telegraph or telephone his stand on the vital problem facing us tonight. Each response will be tabulated as it is received, so that from minute to minute the Congressional leaders here will know, exactly, the sentiments of the majority. Actually this equipment will poll a vote of the whole people tonight on a question of first importance."

The hubbub of the growing crowd carried anew to the listening millions.

"Tomorrow the extraordinary session of Congress called by the President, to consider these momentous measures, will meet. Still in deadlock, they're looking toward this meeting tonight as a final expression of the will of the people. As the millions of Americans respond to the speeches during the evening, so will the Senate and the House of Representatives respond in Washington tomorrow. Never before has the nation waited at such fever heat upon the decision of a question which affects the welfare of every one of us so vitally.

"The leaders of both sides of the issue will be present here tonight. They've come to New York from all points in the nation. They'll listen in on the heartbeat of a nation through this unprecedented polling arrangement. The crowd continues to mob into the building in ever increasing numbers. Soon there won't be a seat left, nor a spot available to stand. The city's entire police force is struggling to handle this great crowd. Minute by minute you'll hear the progress of this gigantic meeting now gathering. Stand by, ladies and gentlemen of the radio audience! Hear the destiny of a nation decided!"

THE WORDS of the radio announcer sounded softly in a black room in the center of the metropolis. In all the world there was no other assembly of men such as the group which listened intently here. A dim light shown upon the black-draped walls of the room, upon their masked faces as they stood silent, motion-less. Secretly they had gathered; secretly they were preparing to act.

The Hidden Hundred had met.

The eyes of the silent men, shining uncannily in the sockets of their skull masks, looked upon the masked face of their leader. He stood behind a black table, facing them, as the voice of the announcer continued to paint the picture of the growing mass meeting in Times Square Garden. His voice carried quietly and firmly:

"It's true, comrades. The very destiny of a nation rests upon the response of the people tonight. The demands of the millions must be answered. If they rise to crush down the Armament Measures, our work has been in vain. The Hidden Hundred must bow before them, like Congress, like the President, if their voice demands defeat of the defense program.

"But—subversive powers have acted upon them. The same subversive powers may strike again tonight to defeat the measures, with some desperate subterfuge, if the people speak approval. Against that we must be on guard. To defeat any attempt to control the will of the people is our purpose tonight. Toward that end we are prepared to dare any danger—pay with our lives if need be. We, we alone, can battle this damnable espionage ring. Upon our success tonight history must hinge.

"Comrades of the Hidden Hundred, you received your orders. Until the proper moment comes, we must wait."

The masked leader turned, parted the black drapes, stepped through them. He passed through black doors, until he reached a small room at the rear of the secret rendezvous. He bolted it. There he stripped off his claw gloves and his skull mask. In a shaded light, Operator 5 took up the telephone and dialed the number of Address Y.

"Dad!" he exclaimed when the voice of ex-Operator Q-6 answered. "You've had no word from Diane?"

"None!" John Christopher answered huskily. "God knows what's happened to her!"

"Stand by that phone, Dad!" Operator 5 said tightly. "Lord, it's almost twenty-four hours now since she—" He broke off. "Ring me at the number I gave you, just as soon as you hear!"

"I will, my boy! Listen! I've just had a call from Tim Donovan. He's still following your orders, watching the Garden. What he told me promises danger—and yet we can't know"

"What did he tell you?"

"Tim believes workmen have been tunneling under the Garden from an abandoned freight subway. He's seen broken stone trucked away and boxes carried into a building nearby which must connect with the secret excavation. The boxes are painted so their labels can't be read, but Tim believes they contain dynamite. What can it mean, Jimmy?"

Operator 5 answered tersely: "I dare not say! Stay by that phone, Dad. God—if only Di could get some word through!"

Jimmy Christopher replaced the instrument. He rose, paced back and forth across the little room. Beyond, his men were awaiting the order to begin their planned actions. Across the city, thousands were mobbing upon Times Square Garden. Minute by minute the time for the beginning of the great mass meeting was approaching....

OVER THE metropolis an electrical tension tightened—and even the girl held prisoner in an isolated turret above Riverside Drive felt the tingle of its import.

In that tiny space Diane Elliot moved about nervously. Through the window she looked upon the twinkling light of the city, the glistening black width of the Hudson. Since she had been thrown into this room the door had not opened once. Her hunger was a growing pain; fatigue throbbed through her body; anxiety had not allowed her any sleep. Beyond the door she heard the sounds of mysterious activity while she remained a forgotten prisoner in the tower.

She peered out, at another window which opened in the sheer wall beyond the corner. It faced hers at right angles, four feet distant. In the room beyond she heard voices speaking faintly, had seen movements. Lights had been burning in it almost constantly; but now, as she watched, they blinked out.

Her gaze had gone again and again to the window, in a hopeless hope. For, just beyond the sill sat a desk, and on the desk rested a telephone. She had seen the well-kept hands of a man moving over the blotter as he worked at the desk, sometimes using the instrument. Now the hands were gone, the room darkened; and the telephone sat in sight, yet out of reach beyond empty space.

Out of reach? She struggled again with the problem of how she might possibly reach it. Through both windows, somehow— she knew it was impossible to bring her hand close enough to touch it. Even if, somehow, she could drag it out of the other window—she could not possibly spin the dial to call a number.

The evident impossibility only spurred her mind on. Her eyes, as they had scores of times, searched the room for some implement by which she might—

Her eyes widened, suddenly. She climbed to the sill of her window and lifted the roller blind from its fixture. Her blood tingling, she unrolled the blind, ripped it from the rod. She turned again to the window. Raising the sash, sitting on the sill, gripping the frame with one hand, she leaned out and reached with the other, pushing the stick toward the pane beyond which the telephone sat.

The far end of the rod touched the lower end of the sash. She scarcely breathed as she tried to pry it into the crack, to force the sash upward. Beneath her, as she worked, yawned empty space. The hand which supported her, curled around the window-frame, ached with tension. To lose her balance would mean a plunge down the sheer wall to—certain death. Leaning far out, she tried breathlessly to poke the window open.

Her efforts infinitesimally widened the crack. And once it widened, it gave more easily. Working the rod like a lever, her eyes shining hopefully now, she slid the sash upward four inches—six—eight. Once the opening was large enough to pass the telephone, she drew back her breath pumping, forced to rest. Then, again, she leaned backward out the window, reaching with her rod, straining every muscle to keep her balance while attempting to slide the telephone toward the sill.

SHE FOUND it impossible to pull the instrument toward her with the stick. Again she drew back, momentarily baffled. On sudden thought she drew hairpins from her hair. One she twisted tightly around an end of the rod, and the protruding end she fashioned into a small hook. Eagerly again she leaned out, and reached through the other window. She drew the hook upon the cord near the base of the instrument; and when she pulled, the telephone slid toward her.

It crossed the sill, dropped. The transmitter fell from its standard and dangled by the cord. She heard the faint buzz in the receiver which meant the line was opened, waiting for the dialing of a number. The telephone was useless to her unless, somehow, she could get the transmitter into her hand. Again she reached with the hook, far down, attempting to catch the lower cord.

Her feet slipped, she tottered on the sill. White-faced, she strained to regain balance. Tightening her grip, she reached again. This time her hook caught the cord connecting the base and the transmitter. Carefully she pulled it toward her. She was forced to free her other hand—the one which kept her balance—in order to reach with it. When she drew back, the blood pounding in her ears, she held the transmitter-receiver while, from the taut cord, the base of the instrument dangled in space between the two windows.

Now she could bring the receiver to her ear, the transmitter to her lips—but the dial was out of reach. Balancing again on the sill, she strove to touch it, but the effort was futile. She knew at once that an attempt to spin the dial with the end of the stick was hopeless…. Then she remembered and her eyes shone with new hope.

Carefully she reached with the stick so that she could press it on the contact bar of the standard. Quickly, ten times, she broke the contact. She waited anxiously, knowing that her action was the equivalent mechanically of dialing the zero. Forty-five seconds ticked past like an eternity. Then, like a voice from heaven, the exchange operator spoke over the line.

"What number did you call, please?"

Diane whispered into the transmitter the number of the telephone at Address Y. "Get it quickly!" She scarcely breathed as she waited. "Will you hang up, please, and dial the number again?" the operator said automatically. "No, no!" the girl blurted. "I can't! Get it for me! Please!" Then again an agonized wait—until a man's voice rasped over the line, the voice of John Christopher. She called his name, whispered her own.

"Di! Good Lord!"

"Listen, Dad!" She spoke in a feverish rush. "I'm being held in the penthouse on Riverside Drive!" Quickly she added the number. "It's the headquarters of the espionage ring, of which Basil Van Praag is the leader. He's here!"

"Van Praag!"

"Yes! Tell Jimmy, Dad! He suspected it long ago, and now it's certain. Van Praag's power is behind it all! Never mind about me, but tell Jimmy!"

"I'll ring him the instant the wire's open!"

"Now, Dad! Now!"

She reached desperately to depress the contact bar of the standard and break the connection. She allowed the telephone to drop against the outside wall. Muscles aching, she endeavored, with the hooked rod, to lift the instrument and replace it on the desk. After a score of tries she abandoned that move as altogether hopeless.

She backed breathlessly from the yawning black space, know-

Operator 5's warning
did not stop the master
spy's darting death!

ing now that if anyone entered the other room and found the telephone dangling over the sill, it would betray the fact that she had sent warning....

ACROSS THE city, in Address Y, ex-Operator Q-6 rapidly dialed a number—the one Jimmy Christopher had given him. His blood thudded while he waited for the connection to go through. When the voice of Operator 5 answered, John Christopher spoke rapidly, breathlessly. His startling message completed, he slammed the instrument down, snatched up his hat, dashed for the door, and hurried out....

Many blocks away, Operator 5 rose tensely from the telephone in the little black room at the rear of the headquarters of the Hidden Hundred. With the words of his father still ringing in his ears, he swiftly drew on skull mask and skeleton gloves. He strode rapidly along a black hallway, flicked aside black curtains and stepped into the room where the clan of living skeletons waited.

They faced him alertly—men whose faces were apparently mere skulls, whose hands were bony claws. Silently they stood, looking into the blazing eyes in the white sockets of their leader's head; and during a moment's hush, the voice of the radio spoke, penetrating a dull roar.

"The great crowd is giving a deafening ovation, ladies and gentlemen, to the speaker who has just been announced. Now the great mass meeting has actually begun. The first plea in this momentous debate is about to be spoken. The deafening cheering you hear, ladies and gentlemen, greets that great champion of disarmament, that statesman who is zealously opposed to the passage of the Armament Bills—Assistant Secretary of State Randolph Morten!"

Operator 5's voice crackled into the roar issuing from the radio.

"Comrades of the Hidden Hundred! Orders!"

CHAPTER 11
SKELETONS IN ACTION

A TAXI sped up Riverside Drive under imperative directions given the driver by the grim-faced passenger. The famous thoroughfare was almost deserted; all New York had moved in mass concentration around Times Square and the great auditorium in which the destiny of a nation was being made tonight. Past red lights the cab fled, to pull up at last with creaking brakes. From it, as he tossed a banknote to the driver, Operator 5 alighted. In one hand he carried the mysterious case he had stolen from himself as Carleton Victor.

He stood rigid, peering at the rising facade of the building, seeing a gleam of windows at its peak. Stepping toward the entrance, he heard quick footfalls and turned to see a gaunt-faced man striding toward him—John Christopher.

"Dad!" he exclaimed. "You're taking a chance by—"

"I couldn't stay back, my boy!" ex-Operator Q-6 exclaimed. "I'm with you on this to the end!"

Jimmy Christopher's lips tightened. "There's not a moment to waste, Dad. Stick with me, if you insist—but be prepared for any danger."

191

Operator 5 shot a quick glance up and down the drive. He glimpsed a parade of taxi cabs drawing rapidly closer. They were swinging toward the curb; men were alighting from them. They began gathering toward the apartment house, from side streets, from a score of points along the Drive, as Jimmy Christopher stepped into the foyer. Tensely, after touching the elevator button, he waited. His nerves went tight as the grille slid open.

He stepped in and ordered: "All the way to the top—as fast as you can make it!"

"I can't take you up, sir, without announcing you. Very strict orders and—"

Jimmy Christopher's hand flicked inside his coat and reappeared gripping an automatic. The startled attendant recoiled.

"Up—fast!" came the ringing command. A gloved hand closed on the control switch. Grimly Jimmy Christopher faced the dismayed operator while he passed his case to his father. "Keep hold of that, until I need it, Dad!" Floor after floor flicked past; and at last, automatically, the cab slowed.

"Take charge of this car, Dad," Jimmy Christopher directed quietly. "Ask no questions of the men who come up—but get them up as rapidly as possible."

Slowly he slid the grille open, stepped alertly into the luxurious reception room. His automatic was holstered now. He turned toward a door as it opened and peered at the rat-eyed manservant who approached.

"You have an appointment, sir?"

"I have," Operator 5 said tightly, "and I'm keeping it now—in a very special way."

He stepped forward threateningly and the hand of the started sentry flashed to his hip. Jimmy Christopher's right hand shot out in a lightning swift blow. His stiff fingertips struck to the throat of the other man as a gun glittered in the light. A hot gasp sounded. Instantly the manservant's body went rigid. Operator 5 caught him as he toppled, lowering him quietly to the Persian rug. Knowing his jiu-jitsu had rendered this man unconscious for the better part of an hour, he straightened, peering at the doors which walled the reception room.

He tried several, found them locked; and peered into two empty rooms. He sensed movement beyond another. He turned from it as a whirring sound came from the elevator shaft; signaled silence as the grille quietly opened. John Christopher was at the cage's controls, and out of it stepped, quickly, fifteen grave-faced men.

THEY MADE no sound as they brought masks from their pockets and drew them over their heads, as they pulled on white-painted gloves. A moment transformed them from men into apparitions. Their claw-like hands drew guns. They waited tensely as Jimmy Christopher reached again for the knob of the door behind which he had heard movements. He tensed himself as a voice came through quietly.

"Tonight we taste victory! Tonight we doom the United States to everlasting helplessness. I'm going now to watch the American people sentence their own nation to destruction!"

Steps came toward the door. Operator 5's quick moves flicked his own mask from his pocket. He drew it on quickly, tugged into his gloves. Near the door the footfalls paused, and a second voice said:

"The Master has already left. He's taken pains that no one will recognize him. He's planned well. Yes—we are prepared for any emergency!"

The knob turned; suddenly the door opened. Light streamed through; a man stepped to the sill and stopped short. Rigid, frozen with consternation, he stared into the reception room—at the figures with skulls for heads.

A strangled cry broke from him as he retreated a step, grabbing toward an arm-pitted gun.

"Don't touch it, Zastrow!"

Operator 5's ringing warning did not stop the darting hand of the master spy. He leaped back as Jimmy Christopher's automatic flashed out. Twice shots blazed. Slugs whipped across the library beyond as the thin-faced man at the desk leaped up. Operator 5 snapped, "Stay back!" to his men and bounded through. Again bullets spat—a fusillade rocked the room.

A bullet from Jimmy Christopher's gun crashed into the light overhead. Only the green-shaded lamp on the desk remained burning, filling the library with a dim reflected glow. At the desk the thin man straightened convulsively, clawing at his throat. His fingers dripped with blood gushing from a wound in his throat. He whirled behind the shelter of the desk, firing swiftly—and suddenly Operator 5 staggered and toppled.

Zastrow rose tensely. "God!" broke from his numbed lips. He aimed to fire into the prone body of the masked Jimmy Christopher; but a sudden terror turned him. He sped into the

194

next room, touched the secret wall-button which slid the huge oil-painting aside. He leaped into the hidden elevator and the panel closed again.

He was not aware that Jimmy Christopher's sharp gaze had followed his every move. Operator 5 sprang up instantly—unhurt. His fall to the floor had been a subterfuge to trick Zastrow into a retreat which might reveal just such secret recesses. Now, his one gloved hand jerking the door wide, he commanded: "Take charge!" The elevator grille opened again, allowing a second squad of the Hidden Hundred to crowd forth. He spun and raced after Zastrow.

His fingers sought the secret contact and found it. The panel slid aside again to reveal the automatically operated cab. He stepped through, paused, held the panel open, snapped a command. A moment later the Morocco leather case was brought to him, and two men came to his side. Then the painting slipped into its socket, and the secret elevator rose.

BLANK WALL slid downward. Slowly the car crawled upward. It stopped. Before the eyes of Operator 5 and his two masked assistants, the panel parted. He stepped forward, placing his case on the floor directly outside, peering at the door. Beyond sat an elaborate desk—the desk at which Diane Elliot had seen the great Basil Van Praag sitting. Now it was deserted. And into the room from the connecting doors there came, with a sudden rush, hard-faced men, guns gripped in their hands.

Jimmy Christopher's automatic blazed defiance. The automatics in the hands of the skeleton men at his side blasted into the roars of the enemy's challenging guns. Lead beat upon the

195

men who charged from the doors. Slugs whistled across the desk of Van Praag with such fury that the attackers were driven backward. Operator 5 whirled as the men retreated through the doors, commanded: "Close them in!"

His gun spat its last bullet, flashing fear into the eyes of crouching men beyond a doorway, as he gripped the knob and pulled. He twisted the key in the lock. His two comrades in the Hidden Hundred were backing from two other doors. Bullets cracked through, splinters flew as Operator 5 shifted to a corner, eyes alert.

From an inner pocket he brought a clip to replace the empty one in his automatic, ordered his men to remain on watch, then moved toward the one door in the wall which had not opened. His hand twisted the knob alertly; he peered through. Deep in a long, dimly lighted corridor, he saw two figures hovering side by side. They were peering at the opening door, automatics in their hands.

Tomas Zastrow's eyes gleamed cruelly; Mayla Lazare's beautiful face was a mask. Through his weird cowl Operator 5 studied them. He straightened, his own automatic held low yet levelly. Deliberately, coldly, he opened the door wide. He stepped directly into the corridor, in full view of the two spies—a being who seemed to be a clothed, living skeleton. With slow, even steps he strode toward Zastrow and the woman as they peered at him in horror.

"You may drop your guns now," his muffled voice sounded, "or you may choose to die."

The woman's answer was a quick pull of the trigger. A bullet blasted along the length of the hallway; nipped at Jimmy Christopher's arm. His slow steps did not stop. His gaze did not flicker. Like a harbinger of doom he glided closer to the terrorized pair; and suddenly the automatic in his clawed hand spat. A scream broke from the lips of Mayla Lazare as she felt her automatic torn from her fingers by a magic power. She sprang away.

She left her automatic lying on the carpet, scarred by the bullet which had struck it, and flung herself into the nearest room. Operator 5's advance went on inexorably. From the bony sockets of his skull head his gleaming eyes shone at Zastrow. The lean spy was straightening, tensing for the moment that would bring death—death to him, or death to the apparition drifting toward him. Horror stiffened his trigger finger as he pointed his weapon directly at Operator 5's heart. And Jimmy Christopher, his own gun twinkling in the light, advanced....

"Now, Zastrow!" he challenged "Now!"

With a wild impulse Zastrow jerked at the trigger. Flame blazed from the automatic, thundering into the report that came at the same instant from the gun in the clawed hand. It lighted his widened eyes as they followed the clothed skeleton's quick move against the wall. His jaw dropped as a whining breath passed into his lungs; his automatic spun from his fingers; stupidly he peered down at the tiny black hole directly above his heart.

Then he fell. He was dead as he hit the floor.

THE GHOSTLY figure with the skull head whirled and peered along the corridor. "Diane!" came through the fabric of his mask. He strode swiftly; he stopped short as he heard a startled answer: "Jimmy! Jimmy!" It led him to a door; he twisted the knob and found it firm, the keyhole empty. "Steady, Di!" His gloved hand moved toward the pocket in which he kept his pack of master keys.

An explosion of voices beyond the outer door startled him. Quick footfalls sounded. He turned to see masked men crowding in, and among them, amazed by the sight of the weird figures, John Christopher. Ex-Operator Q-6 strode at the side of an alert figure who spoke ringingly to Operator 5.

"We're trapped, captain! Intelligence men are in the lobby, sir—coming up! Z-7s with them! We're holding them back, but it's only a question of seconds—"

"Mass against them!" Operator 5 commanded. "Don't fire a shot—but you've got to break past! We've got them at a disadvantage—there can't be many because most of them are at the Garden tonight! My case, X-1! Take charge!"

X-1 whirled to follow orders. Quickly Operator 5 turned to the door on which Diane's hands were pounding. John Christopher stared at him in dismay as he bared his master keys. Quickly he hammered at the bolt, drew it back. One of his lieutenants pressed his case into his hands as he twisted the knob and stepped through.

Diane Elliot backed in unbounded surprise as the strange figure with the skull head entered. She peered past at John Christopher, and he hurried to her side. Fascinated, they watched the quick movements of the captain of the Hidden Hundred. Near the window he was opening his case.

From a compartment inside he whisked a coil of thin silken

rope. Quickly he knotted one end of it around the radiator under the window; then tossed the coil outward. It snaked into the darkness as he turned and commanded crisply:

"Down!"

John Christopher urged as the girl hesitated: "You've got to do it, Di! Z-7's coming up! If he sees you here—if he connects you with the spy ring, it means—"

"Down!" the command rang again, more sharply.

Diane's face went white as she hurried to the sill. She gripped the rope in her trembling hands and mounted to the sill. Eyes flickering at the dread figure with the skull head, she lowered herself. Her breath stopped as she slid downward, peering at the light of the window above. She dared not glance into the chasm of darkness below. Hands aching, body throbbing with the effort, she lowered herself with desperate quickness—while the skull head peered down at her.

Operator 5 stepped back quickly and signaled John Christopher. "After her, sir! Quickly!" Ex-Operator Q-6 did not hesitate. From the outer offices the sound of quickly moving feet was audible, the gruff mingling of voices. Snatches of sentences indicated that Z-7 and the Intelligence men had entered the lower offices; that a fight was in progress between the service men and the Hidden Hundred. He peered down, saw that Diane had disappeared in the darkness of the court, and closed his hands tightly on the rope.

JIMMY CHRISTOPHER peered down until his father became almost invisible in the gloom below. Through the door behind him came a startled: "Hurry it, captain! Z-7's coming up on the special elevator!" Operator 5 swung over the sill. He coiled the rope around his legs and slid. Windows flashed past him. While he was still descending he felt a vibration through the rope, and peered up.

On the sill of the high window a woman was poised. Mayla Lazare. Her face white with terror, her skirts fluttering in the wind, she snatched at the tightrope. She balanced herself precariously as ringing voices behind warned her of imminent capture. Hands wrapped on the rope, she lowered herself out of the light. It slipped through her fingers and burned; the very pain made it impossible for her to grip it more tightly. With increasing speed she slid downward; Operator 5, far below, heard a scream of terror tear from her lips.

Her hands were burned to the bone against the thin strand. Another scream tore from her lips as she plummeted. Jimmy Christopher saw her shadow fluttering against the side of the building while she plunged. His feet struck the cement of the court and he whirled away with a gasp. An instant later there was a violent, sickening thud as the body of Mayla Lazare bounced alongside. The plunge must have broken every bone in her body.

The figure with the skull head whirled. One of his clawed hands snatched the wrist of the terrorized Diane Elliot. John Christopher hurried after them as they hastened to an entrance in the basement of the building. There, in light shining faintly through a pebbled pane, Jimmy Christopher paused.

Quickly he snatched off his gloves, pulled the skull mask from his head. He noted the dismay in his father's eyes, the rush of color to Diane's face; and a grim smile tightened his lips.

"Jimmy!" the girl blurted. "Van Praag—gave me the job of finding the leader of the Hidden Hundred—thinking I was Mayla Lazare—and the leader is you!"

"Yes, Di."

"Good God, Jimmy!" John Christopher blurted. "The whole Service is ordered to get you! You're risking everything—"

"Because it's the only way, Dad! I'm asking no quarter and giving none. The Hidden Hundred is fighting this out to the end!"

Ex-Operator Q-6 stared. "The fact that you're their leader, my boy, completely vindicates them in my mind! Listen—the Secretary of State has refused my services. I can't stay idle. I offer myself—if you'll have me—as a member of the Hidden Hundred!"

Operator 5's eyes lighted. "There's at least one vacancy now, Dad. God knows how many there'll be after tonight—but now there's at least one, that of the man who was once D-4 of the Intelligence, who became X-13 of the Hidden Hundred. His place is yours if you'll have it—and I'll be proud to have you at my side."

"I accept, Jimmy!"

Tightly ex-Operator Q-6 gripped hands with the man whose life was masked under so many identities. His clasp pledged his devotion to Operator 5, to Carleton Victor, to Huntley Walsh—and, in eternal faith, to his son, the leader of the Hidden Hundred.

CHAPTER 12
A NATION SPEAKS

E VERY STREET leading to the great Times Square Garden was choked with cars, thronged with multitudes. Every available bit of standing space was filled. Heads peered from the open windows of surrounding buildings; stoops were piled with people; hundreds stood or sat on the tops of cars caught in a swamp of traffic. The major part of New York's police force struggled vainly to clear the ways. Thousands crushed in the mob and cheered the voice issuing from the public address system installed to carry into the streets.

The tones of Assistant Secretary of State Randolph Morten rang out resonantly.

"The millions we would spend on armament are a means of committing national suicide. The very fortification of our bases in the Pacific are lighting the fires of war!* Let us not burn our millions in the furnace of armed conflict. Let us use them to

---

* AUTHOR's NOTE: Berths for the Navy's mightiest men-of-war and bases for its submarines and aircraft were recommended in a far-flung $38,000,000 building program placed before the House Naval Affairs Committee recently. Concentrating naval defense construction in the Pacific danger zone, a bill reported by Chairman Vinson provides:

A floating dry-dock at Pearl Harbor, Hawaii, $10,000,000. Barracks and machine shops, $3,500,000. A graving dry-dock storehouse and time signal station at Mare Island, Cal., $4,300,000. A graving dry-dock and accessories at Puget Sound, Wash., $4,500,000. A submarine base at Coco Solo,

nurture humanity, instead of to destroy it! Let us raise our hands to the world—hands empty of weapons—and declare sincerely that our highest desire is for peace!"

Cheers roared through the crowd as a line of men worked their way desperately along the sidewalk, and fought toward an entrance of the building to which patrolmen opened the way. The foremost of them, flashing credentials, thus led them past packed thousands, into the great hall. Outside the arena he paused and drew them around him.

Operator 5 said quietly: "Join your comrades and take your posts. Keep constantly on the alert!"

The men nodded. Operator 5 left them at once, climbing crowded stairs. He worked his way toward the rear of the platform erected at the one end of the tremendous arena. He paused to study the spectacle of the unprecedented crowd in the huge building.

Every seat in the vast auditorium was taken. In violation of the fire regulations, because the hundreds of firemen had found it impossible to combat the pressure of the mob, thousands more were crowded into the aisles. The four balconies, as well as the arena, were massed. Operator 5's eyes grew dark with dread at

Panamá Canal Zone, $2,534,000; a Coco Solo air base, $420,000. Barracks, magazine and hangars at San Diego air base, $2,500,000.

Revealing that the Chief of Naval Operations had designated the Pearl Harbor dry-dock as No. 1 on the construction priority list, the committee said: "The dock is urgently needed to correct a general lack of properly equipped advanced naval bases."

the thought of what terrible disaster would result if terror should strike into the midst of such a crowd....

On the platform, in bright light, addressing the multitude through the public address system, the nation and the world through banks of microphones—Assistant Secretary Morten was speaking. His voice rang loudly and clearly into the reaches of the auditorium, rang with deep-felt fervor.

"A nation does not prepare for any war. It does not prepare for war in general. It prepares for a specific, planned war. That's a fundamental axiom which even our greedy militarists will admit, a truth the whole world knows. The whole world looks upon us now as an aggressor threatening its safety with our plans to rearm—looks upon us with a fear that will grow until inevitably we'll be shedding the blood of our youth in another frightful war which will encompass the world. A war for which the United States must, in all history, be held solely guilty!"

Operator 5 strode closer to the rear of the platform. Out of sight of the crowd he stood, curtained by the hanging bunting, again studying the impressive scene. He brought from his pocket a small, powerful pair of binoculars. He was preparing to use them when a small figure hurried toward him, and a hard hand caught at his arm.

"Jimmy!"

Operator 5 peered at Tim Donovan. "Still on the job, old-timer? Good boy! Have you been watching?"

"I've checked up again, Jimmy! There's something planted in and under this building but the wires are hidden so well they can't be traced!"

"I'm afraid you're right, Tim," Operator 5 agreed quietly. "And if the signal is given…." His voice faded. "Stand by, Tim. I'll need you."

HE RAISED the binoculars and peered through them at the rows upon rows of men and women in the forefront of the audience. At a glance he recognized many of the faces magnified through his lenses—Senators, Representatives, members of the President's cabinet, officers of the Army and Navy, the leaders of great civilian organizations backing the armament program. To these reserved seats had come many men and women whose names were known around the world; and now they were listening intently, solemnly, to the scathing denunciation of the Arms Bills by Assistant Secretary Morten.

Morten's oratory had earned him fame throughout the country. But never before had he swayed a crowd so magically. The thousands sat spellbound as his voice rose, as he approached the climax of his address. Every face was rapt, every eye shining upon the Assistant Secretary.

Jimmy Christopher's lenses showed him scores of Intelligence men on duty in the auditorium, detailed here by the orders of Z-7. Thousands of city policemen were also in evidence, near the exits. Along the fringe of the crowd, alert, eyes sharp, were the faces of those who made up the Hidden Hundred. A grave light shone in Operator 5's eyes as he continued to scan the faces of those nearest the platform. Then, abruptly, his lenses paused.

Their circle now framed a lean face, the eyes shadowed by shaggy brows, the pointed van dyke masking a cruelly thin mouth. Quickly he shifted the glasses to Tim, and directed

Chilled by finding both were blocked, the two men recoiled in terror!

207

the boy to study the same face. His voice was a whisper as he declared:

"Never forget that face, Tim. It's disguised cleverly—but there's no doubt the man behind it is Basil Van Praag! He's one of the most powerful figures in the world—here, tonight, incognito. The man speaking now is his lieutenant. It's Van Praag's work which threatens to defeat the rearmament bill—his leadership of the most dangerous espionage ring that ever operated in the United States!"

The boy drew back, eyes widened in dismay.

"Through the newspapers in Europe, he controls whole governments. His orders can transform his publications into powerful weapons for or against any regime. He's raised bribery to its highest limits—for he collects huge secret sums from the governments he serves. In Europe, his papers have preached armament until now every Power is stronger than ever before. At the same time he's bought control of powerful agencies in this country—the Amalgamated, for instance—and through them has advocated disarmament. Europe to arm! America to disarm! His weapon is a two-edged sword against us!"

The boy glanced past Operator 5, and at another entrance, saw the grim-faced Z-7.

"Van Praag is no doubt making himself the richest and most powerful man in the world—if his tactics to crush the defense measures succeeds. Keep your eye on that man, Tim. Watch his eyes move. If he leaves his seat, follow him, and at the first opportunity report to me. You'll find me either in the wire room, or near the office of Randolph Morten."

"Trust me, Jimmy!"

Z-7'S VOICE grated as he neared Operator 5. "Thank God you've been on the job! I was called off by startling information from MW. One of our operators spotted some of the ex-Intelligence men and trailed them to an apartment house on Riverside Drive. I signaled a raid—and I have to confess a miserable failure. We had two score of the Hidden Hundred trapped, and every one of them escaped us! Their leader among them!"

"Better luck next time, Chief." Operator 5 said it quietly.

"We failed because we were outnumbered. Damned strange! Not a shot was fired against us, and yet those men faced the extreme penalty if they were apprehended. They were acting on orders from their leader, and those orders give me a clue to his identity. I'm going to run that man to earth, Operator 5. I'll never quit this case until I do!"

"I'm positive of that, Chief," Jimmy Christopher answered gravely.

Z-7's black eyes smoldered. He gestured with a hand which held several scribbled notes. "Another strange thing just reported to me by my operator in charge of this detail. The proponents of the armament bills are here in full force. Not one of them has failed to attend. Yet one after another of the big leaders of the disarmament faction have sent their regrets or simply failed to appear."

"I know. Chief," Operator 5 answered. "I've already noticed that. All the leaders in favor of rearming the United States are here, including the Senators and Representatives whose votes must decide the issue at the extraordinary session of Congress tomorrow. If some strange power should strike at them—destroy them tonight—the armament cause would be completely lost."

"What!" Z-7 snapped. "What do you mean by that? What the devil are you driving at?"

"If I explained, you'd think me mad." Jimmy Christopher signaled Tim Donovan and the boy began to sidle away, intent on carrying out his orders to keep the great Basil Van Praag under observation. "Perhaps I'm dead wrong. I hope I am, but—"

He broke off as a tremendous ovation shook the hall. Thousands of voices rose in a deafening cheer. Operator 5 turned to observe the thousands who roared their approval of Randolph Morten's stirring speech. The Assistant Secretary had completed his address. Bowing to the thunder of the mob, he was withdrawing to the rear of the platform.

"God!" Z-7 exclaimed. "Apparently the people are behind him. It can only mean that the armament measures are doomed!"

"Perhaps not, Chief," Operator 5 answered. "The crowd here is only a small fraction of those listening to the speeches. The millions scattered over the country are not a part of this mob, not subject to the spell of mass psychology. They're separate entities, each thinking for himself. It's that response which will tell."

Operator 5 stood quietly until the furor subsided, until the chairman of the great meeting advanced to the microphones. A voice rang out over the crowd:

"Ladies and gentlemen, the champion of the armament cause will address you now. Major-General Falk, Chief of Staff of the United States Army and Navy."

A HUSH filled the hall as General Falk stepped toward the

microphone. He began in a low, modulated voice. His words carried with a ring of sincerity into the great auditorium. Quietly—his voice yet vibrating with power—he began:

"Ladies and Gentlemen, citizens of the United States. I face you with a sense of shame. I am the highest officer, except for my Commander-in-chief, the President, of the armed forces of the United States. The highest officer of the armed forces of the greatest nation on the face of the globe. I face you with a sense of shame because my army—the army which must protect your lives and your homes in a time of national crisis—ranks not the first in the world, as it should, but—sixteenth!"

Operator 5 turned away quietly, leaving Z-7. Mounting a flight of stairs which carried him toward the suites of offices at the front of the great building, he strode directly to the door of the one he knew had been assigned to Randolph Morten and the supporters of the disarmament cause. He opened the door; found it empty; entered, and shot the bolt.

Quickly, he examined the room. Minutes later, when he finished the task, he had found nothing whatever of a suspicious nature.

He stepped from the office, and hurried toward a door at the end of the corridor. Bright light filled it, and a deafening clatter. Men in shirt sleeves were hovering over scores of clicking teletype machines. Girls were working the cams and plugs of a gigantic bank of telephone switchboards. Into this room messages were pouring from all over the United States, from the listening millions. Great baskets were already filled with bundled telegrams and notated slips of the messages already received. And at one end of the room an electrically operated tally board was checking the response.

An Intelligence man stationed near the door spoke above the hubbub. "Morten pulled a tremendous response. The messages started coming in as soon as he began speaking. The influx was almost more than the force could handle. Falk has been speaking five minutes now—and there's scarcely any answer, compared with the Morten count. Of course, we can't tell until the end—messages will be coming in here all night—but perhaps it's an indication."

"Whatever the people decide," Operator 5 answered, "they will speak once and for all tonight."

Jimmy Christopher felt a tug at his arm, and peered down at the wide-eyed Tim Donovan. The boy was breathless as he said: "Van Praag's left his seat, Jimmy! I followed him to Morten's office. Morten saw him go, too, and followed. They're in there together now!"

"Good boy! Now, Tim, an even more important job. Slip away and keep an eye on Z-7. Take this whistle with you." Operator 5 pressed it into the boy's hand. "When you hear a whistled note from somewhere in these offices, repeat it with your own. That's important, Tim. It's a signal—and you mustn't lose a moment doing it!"

"Okay, Jimmy! But what's it for? Why do you want me to watch Z-7?"

"The whistle will signal the Hidden Hundred into action," Operator 5 explained as he walked along the corridor with the boy. "And when they appear, Z-7 and the Intelligence men will be the greatest danger they face. My men are risking everything tonight—and they've got to act at the same instant, as quickly as possible, or they'll be defeated even before they begin."

"Trust me, Jimmy!"

Tim Donovan hurried down a flight of stairs, toward the rear of the platform. Near its edge, Z-7 was standing, listening to the ringing tones of Major-General Falk. The Chief of Staff's voice was vibrant with emotion as he uttered his plea to the crowd. He indulged in no oratory. He stated facts, and in response to them there was no cheering. Solemnly the crowd listened. Z-7 stood aside alone, tense with the electrical charge in the air; and, unobserved, Tim Donovan watched him.

The boy's hand closed hotly on the whistle.

OPERATOR 5 strode quickly toward the door of the office assigned to Randolph Morten. Near it he paused, heard voices speaking in low tones, voices which told him Morten and Van Praag were inside. He moved on, to the adjoining office, stepped into it, and toward a connecting door. Tensely he listened.

A latch clicked as someone entered Morten's office. A husky voice declared: "The response to Falk's speech is coming in now! It's overwhelming! The messages are more than the operators can handle! Within a few moments there'll be a greater tally in favor of the armament bills than we can hope to muster against it!"

"What!"

"It's true, I tell you! It means our cause is lost! There's no other—"

"Go back!" the voice of Morten commanded. "Watch the board! Report again when—"

Operator 5 turned as a quiet knock sounded on the door of his own office. He opened it. Into the room stepped two ex-Intelligence agents. They were X-22 and X-40—men he had assigned to special duty. Worn from the struggle of working their way through the crowd, their reports came in whispers.

"We've checked Tim Donovan's findings, sir. It's true. A tunnel has been excavated under the Garden. It must lead directly to the center of the arena."

"But it's blocked up now, captain," the other answered. "Walled with brick and cement. Something is sealed inside it; and there's no way of reaching it. It would take hours, perhaps a night of work to get beyond the barrier."

"On the open side we found piles of empty boxes—dynamite containers. It can only mean that the sealed cavity is filled with explosive—a vast store of it. We tried to find the detonating wires which connect with the charge, but it's impossible. They lead out from somewhere within the cavity—from some point we can't hope to reach without a long hunt."

"God, captain!" X-22 blurted it "There's nothing we can do to break the connection—wherever it leads!"

Operator 5 nodded tensely. "Good work! Go back to your posts. Await the signal!"

The two members of the Hidden Hundred hurried out. Operator 5 followed them, turning the other way. He ran down a flight of steps. At one side he saw Tim Donovan watching Z-7. The Washington chief was standing behind the raised platform, listening to the words of the Chief of Staff. General Falk was within view at the edge of the platform. Standing aside, Operator 5 studied that platform.

Then he saw it. Above the draped bunting, on a red-white-and-blue crest, so faint that the crowd could not have seen it, so cryptic they could not have dreamed its meaning—a mark that nevertheless stood out in startling relief to the keen eyes of Jimmy Christopher. A symbol hovering above the thousands, promising doom!

The scythe!

CHAPTER 13
THE HIDDEN HUNDRED WAITS

EYES DARKENED, face lined, Operator 5 strode quickly from the platform. He ran up the steps; walked briskly along the corridor; reentered the office beside that of Randolph Morten. Listening at the connecting door, he heard nothing. The men in the other room were waiting tensely, anxiously, for further report on the flood of messages flowing into the wire room in the great building.

Again quick steps came along the corridor; a knock sounded in the room beyond; a door clicked open. The same husky voice brought startling news to the two waiting men.

"The messages are coming in even larger numbers now! The lines can't carry them all. We're overwhelmed! The people are demanding the rearmament of the United States! Tomorrow Congress must vote the bills!"

"Unless—"

The low voice of Van Praag spoke the word. A sharp command from Randolph Morten sent the messenger from the room. Operator 5 knew that now the two men—the Assistant Secretary of State and the powerful newspaper publisher—were facing each other alone. A moment of silence passed before Van Praag completed his ominous sentence.

"Unless the advocates of the armament bill do not live to vote in favor of it!"

"Yes!" Morten whispered. "There's only one way, now, to turn defeat into victory! We must not wait! I'll give the orders!"

"Give them!"

Jimmy Christopher heard the click of a telephone receiver being raised. He heard a dial spin once—and click a connection with the operator. Morten's voice whispered a number into the transmitter in a tone so low Operator 5's keen ears could not catch it. Then Morten's tone became louder as he barked a command:

"Close the switches! In exactly ten minutes! Ten!"

Operator 5 heard the connection broken, heard quick movements. Quickly he drew his pack of master keys from his pocket. With deft, swift movements, none of them audible to the men in the room beyond, he tried two keys. The second silently drew the lock. Then, quickly, he whipped skull mask and skeleton gloves from his pocket and drew them on.

Transformed into a weird apparition, he moved alertly to the hallway door. He brought a shining whistle to his lips; blew a shrill blast upon it. The fluttering sound fell away, and immediately was echoed from a point beyond. Tim Donovan, obeying orders, was relaying the signal.

Operator 5 heard a hush descend into the great hall beyond; and he stepped quickly to the connecting door. His clawed hand jerked it open. He stepped into brighter light. At the sound of his movements, the two men whirled to face him. Randolph Morten jerked from the door. The disguised Van Praag stood rigid with surprise. Operator 5 faced them empty-handed, eyes glittering deeply in the sockets of his skull mask.

"You're about to leave, gentlemen?" he asked quietly. "I must disrupt your plans. You're going to remain here—let there be no doubt of that."

VAN PRAAG jerked a hand in and out of his pocket, raised an automatic. His shadowed eyes gleamed coldly as he moved toward Operator 5. Jimmy Christopher made no gesture to draw a weapon. He stood motionless, eyes hard upon Van Praag.

"Stand aside!" he ordered.

Randolph Morten peered in terror at the clothed skeleton; then jerked to the side of Van Praag. His trembling hand shot to the knob. Van Praag opened the door wide and they started through. On the sill they stopped, frozen.

Peering into the hallway, they saw other figures like the one which had entered upon them. Six such figures, whose heads were skulls, whose hands were claws. And every one of the six was leveling an automatic at the door.

"You will not leave, gentlemen!" Operator 5 declared again quietly.

The two men backed away in terror, slapped the door shut.

They whirled to the connecting way through which the apparition had entered. Again they pulled the door open wide, and again went rigid. Across the sill they saw another squad of the skeleton men. Eyes gleamed at them from bony sockets, automatics swung at them menacingly. Chilled, finding both ways blocked, they recoiled.

Jimmy Christopher thrust the door shut. He faced Morten and Van Praag with gleaming eyes. His voice sounded muffled through his mask.

"You can't possibly leave this building now, gentlemen. Are you convinced of that?"

Morten leaned across the table while Van Praag retreated to the rear wall. The great man's automatic was still in his hand, leveled; yet Operator 5 gave it no heed. The Assistant Secretary blurted:

"Who are you? What do you want?"

The captain of the Hidden Hundred stood with his back squarely against the hallway door. "I'm aware that your secret workers have planted a huge charge of explosives beneath this building," he said. "You are ready to destroy this building and everyone in it as a last extremity. The necessity is upon you now. The people of the United States are demanding stronger defenses. You can defeat them only by destroying their leaders. You have just given the order for the explosive to be discharged in ten minutes!"

Morten straightened defiantly. "You know a great deal, whoever you are—and it's true. There *are* tons of explosive stored beneath this building now—directly beneath the sections in which the leaders of the armament movement are sitting! There are wires connecting with it, leading to a building blocks away. I've just called that building by telephone. When the ten minutes are up, the switches will be closed. Nothing you can do will stop that!"

"Perhaps," Operator 5's quiet voice answered. "But you stipulated a wait of ten minutes, Mr. Morten, in order to give yourself and Van Praag time to get out of the building. Your one thought is to save yourselves. I am, you see, keeping you here for an excellent reason. If this building is destroyed, you will be destroyed with it!"

Morten snapped: "And you!"

"That," the voice came hollowly from the skull, "is of no moment. I'm quite willing to accept the end. Gentlemen—are you? You seem anxious. Your faces are pale. You are trembling. You wish to escape the building—and you cannot. You do not wish to die—and you face death now, with the thousands who are here. Accept it as a certainty, gentlemen—you will perish with the rest, on your own orders—unless you countermand them!"

Morten snapped: "I will not do that! I'm willing to give my life for this cause! My orders stand, whether I remain or go! If it must be—we shall all die when the ten minutes have ended!"

OPERATOR 5 said quietly: "The time is passing rapidly, gentlemen. Even if you don't change your orders, you'll not achieve your purpose. You'll cause the deaths of thousands of innocent persons, but you'll not destroy the leaders of the arms bills. For gentlemen, at this very moment they are leaving the building, escorted by the Hidden Hundred. They're being led to safety—and if your explosive destroys this building and the thousands in it, the important leaders will remain alive to vote the passage of the defense measures tomorrow!"

"That's not true!"

"I assure you—the muffled voice carried absolute conviction—"it *is* the truth."

They listened through the door and heard a muffled roaring of the crowd—an ominous rumble in which the voice of no speaker was discernible. Through the building some audible tension grew second by second, testifying that in the great auditorium something strange was occurring....

At the repeated blast of the whistle General Falk had been startled into silence. The next moment a hush had fallen into the great auditorium—because every light had blinked out. Complete darkness had filled the huge hall for a moment, until bright spots of light appeared on all sides. Electric torches, the beams of which disclosed a startling sight.

Magically, throughout the vast room, weird figures appeared. Their heads were skulls from which determined eyes gleamed. Their clawed hands waved automatics. Their muffled commands struck terror into the hearts of the thousands. Swiftly, moving in accordance with a carefully prearranged plan, they went into action.

Backs to the closed doors, they barred egress. Their lights played into the eyes of policemen, firemen, Intelligence operators, blinding them. Others fought their way through the crowd toward the platform; and hundreds shrank back in dismay to allow them passage. They crowded upon the dignitaries near the front—the men in whose hands lay the fate of the armament bills. Upon the platform one of the Hidden Hundred leaped, springing toward the bank of microphones.

Z-7 sprang into startled action the moment the flickering torches disclosed the skeletal heads of the Hidden Hundred. Driven by a cold fury, he started for the rear of the platform. The public address system offered him a means of shouting urgent orders to his men. He raced to the steps—and stopped short.

Blinding light stabbed into his eyes. Skull heads appeared before him. Guns glimmered in his direction. A ringing voice commanded:

"Stay back! We're in charge here!"

Z-7 found himself completely surrounded by the apparitions, closed in by a ring of guns. The phantoms pressed upon him. Claw-like hands gripped his arms and held him motionless. In grim fury, hopelessly, he tried to break away. He ceased his struggling when a voice boomed through the auditorium—the voice of the member of the Hidden Hundred who had leaped to the microphones.

"Ladies and gentlemen! Do not be alarmed! Do not give way to panic! Obey my instructions implicitly! Leave your seats quietly, without hurrying! Those in the aisles go to the nearest exits. All others follow in good order! If you conduct yourselves calmly you will soon be out of the building. Follow the directions of the men in the masks!"

A STIRRING answered the startling voice. Near the front of the auditorium bright lights were playing, and the eyes of thou-

221

sands turned upon the gleam. The commands of the Hidden Hundred had forced out row upon row of persons. From their seats officers of the Army and Navy, Congressmen, civic leaders, were filing. Guided by the Hidden Hundred, those upon whom the fate of the nation rested were being conducted away first from the waiting danger.

Z-7 in the hands of the skeleton figures, realized that his small detail of men was outnumbered. The entire hall was under the command of the Hidden Hundred. Under the orders of the masked figures it began to empty. Hundreds and thousands began streaming into the streets, and the crowds outside to surge away under their advancing pressure. The gleaming lights disclosed white faces, terrorized eyes—and yet none of the thousands knew the doom that was lurking beneath them.

The tramping of feet sounded muffled in the office of Randolph Morten. At the door Operator 5 stood backed. Facing him across the table stood the grim Assistant Secretary. At the far wall the disguised Van Praag stood rigid. Quietly Jimmy Christopher glanced at his watch, and his voice sounded muffled again.

"The time now is very short."

A knock sounded at the door behind him. A voice called in quickly: "Captain! The armament crusaders are out of the building! The auditorium is half emptied! In a few moments they'll all be out!"

Operator 5 nodded with grim satisfaction. "You hear, gentlemen?" he inquired. "Now, what is your decision? To die under your own orders for a lost cause? You must decide quickly. You have now one minute. Sixty seconds—beginning to tick away as I speak!"

The desperate eyes of Randolph Morten narrowed. Suddenly he lifted the telephone. His lean finger spun the zero of the dial. He whispered a number into the transmitter. Eyes glittering upon Operator 5, he spoke tersely as the connection went through.

"Verifying orders! Your ten minutes are almost up! Close the switches on the moment! Close them—"

A sharp crack! The automatic in the hand of Van Praag spat flame. A bullet whistled across the room. The report reverberated deafeningly as Operator 5 tightened, eyes upon the powerful figure standing against the wall. Smoke wisped from the gun in his hand as Morten, at the table, emitted a sigh. The Assistant Secretary bent forward, slid to the floor. The telephone dropped from his hand.

Van Praag sprang desperately toward the instrument, snatched it up. His lips worked stiffly near the transmitter.

"The Master speaking! Orders! Final order! Do not close the switches! Do not explode the charge! Do you hear? In God's name, don't—"

Out of the receiver a voice rang. "Orders from the Master! Switches off!"

Van Praag flung the telephone away. Face contorted with fury, he crept toward the door. His gun held on Operator 5 as he reached for the knob. Suddenly he jerked the door wide and sped through.

In the corridor, skull-masked men closed upon Van Praag as

the great man lunged and broke through their ranks, stumbling down the steps, fleeing in terror. The skeletal figures crowded after him, hastily.

Operator 5 turned, stooped, peered at the white face of Randolph Morten. The Assistant Secretary was dead. He moved quickly then, hurrying across the corridor, down the steps, where, in the gleaming light of the torches, he now saw Van Praag recoiling in terror—surrounded by men whose heads were fleshless skulls.

Van Praag retreated slowly, step by step, as the ghastly ring of clothed skeletons tightened around him. Suddenly he whirled, sprang up the steps leading to the platform. He dashed across it—and again stopped. Swinging beams showed him that the great auditorium was almost empty. All around the platform phantom figures were posted, their eyes gleaming, their guns flashing. Von Praag whirled, saw them advancing on all sides. A cry of anguish burst from his lips....

He raised his gun. The flame singed the dyed hair at his temple. He plunged headlong to the boards, and lay still. The red of his blood colored the wood beneath him as a sharp command rang from the masked lips of the captain of the Hidden Hundred.

When the clawed hands released Z-7, when his bellowed orders brought his men running toward him and returned light to the vast auditorium, he peered around through the emptiness—emptiness from which the Hidden Hundred had fled.

On the platform Basil Von Praag lay dead beneath the symbol

of the scythe. And the shot that killed him had been heard around the world....

INTO THE ears of a waiting, anxious nation, news flashed from Washington, D.C.

> CONGRESS PASSES ARMS BILLS!
>
> STRENGTHENING OF NATION'S DEFENSES BEGINS!
>
> UNITED STATES OVERWHELMINGLY SUPPORTS VITAL MEASURES!
>
> PRESIDENT SIGNS BILLS AT ONCE!
>
> TASK RUSHED TO RAISE U.S. TO FIRST IN ARMED STRENGTH!

The news carried into every cranny of the country; and into the secret rooms which comprised the central headquarters of the United States Intelligence. In the office of the Washington chief, as the result of the Congressional vote was flashed, stood Z-7, Operator 5, and the Secretary of State.

Z-7's black eyes were smouldering; the Secretary's face was drawn with cold wrath; and a tight, wry smile tugged at the corners of Jimmy Christopher's mouth.

"Thank God!" the chief exclaimed. "No longer will we be the weakling of the world! I wish to say to you, Mr. Secretary, that this result gratifies me to the depths of my soul. At the same time, I have to add that I've strictly followed your orders."

"I am aware that you have," the Secretary said coldly. "I am also aware that you have failed to break up the Hidden Hundred and failed to apprehend its leader. My orders to you still stand, Z-7. You will concentrate on this case. You will exert every resource to crush that organization. You will capture that unknown leader. Once we have him, he can suffer only one penalty—death!"

Grimly Z-7 answered. "I'll follow your orders, sir."

"And if you do not succeed," the Secretary snapped, "I'll take you out of command and put a man in your place who *will* get results!"

Operator 5's face paled as the Secretary stamped from the office. Z-7, eyes grim, lifted from his desk a typed letter which had come only that morning. He reread it as he held it in trembling fingers.

"A message from the leader of the Hidden Hundred!" he snapped. "The daring of the man! Informing me that no one in the organization is responsible for the death of T-6. Assuring me their only purpose has been to help their country. Regardless of that, my boy, I'm going to fight that organization with all the strength of the Intelligence—until it is destroyed!"

"Yes, Chief." Operator 5 answered in a low tone.

"I'm going to concentrate on finding evidence to prove the identity of the leader of the Hidden Hundred. I'm too old in this game, Operator 5, to make a move against him without strong evidence to back me up. I have none now—but I'm going to get it! When I do, it can result only in the death of that subversive leader!"

"Yes, sir!"

"That's all," Z-7 finished quietly. But as Operator 5 turned tensely to the door: "Except—I've heard that pebbles placed inside the cheeks will alter the tone of the voice so that it's not recognizable. That's a point the leader of the Hidden Hundred had better heed!"

Z-7's eyes were glittering now. Jimmy Christopher searched them intently. But again he turned quietly, without speaking. As he passed through the secret doors, the voice of the Secretary of State carried through his mind.

"The penalty… death!"

IN THE black-draped room, under the cover of night, at a remote point in Washington, a strange meeting was being held. In silent rows stood men whose heads were fleshless skulls, whose hands were the hands of skeletons. They faced their leader and listened intently to his firm voice.

Through his skull mask the eyes of Operator 5 studied the masked faces before him. One, he knew, was his father, ex-Operator Q-6, now designated X-13. All of them were loyal, fearless—soldiers of secrecy sworn to the defense of their nation. He spoke to them quietly.

"Comrades of the Hidden Hundred, our task is completed. To you and to you alone the credit of a great victory must go. I thank you all from the bottom of my heart. Let's never forget that we are bound in secrecy, that ours must be an undying purpose though death strike into our ranks…. Comrades of the Hidden Hundred, hold yourselves ready for further orders!

"Dismiss!"

227